D0345486

Also by
JULEAH DEL ROSARIO

*500 Words or Less*

# Turtle Under Ice

Juleah del Rosario

**SIMON PULSE**

New York  London  Toronto  Sydney  New Delhi

SIMON PULSE
An imprint of Simon & Schuster Children's Publishing Division
1230 Avenue of the Americas, New York, New York 10020
First Simon Pulse hardcover edition February 2020
Text copyright © 2020 by Juleah Swanson
Jacket illustration copyright © 2020 by Adams Carvalho
All rights reserved, including the right of reproduction in whole or in part in any form.
SIMON PULSE and colophon are registered trademarks of Simon & Schuster, Inc.
For information about special discounts for bulk purchases, please contact
Simon & Schuster Special Sales at 1-866-506-1949 or business@simonandschuster.com.
The Simon & Schuster Speakers Bureau can bring authors to your live event.
For more information or to book an event contact the Simon & Schuster Speakers Bureau
at 1-866-248-3049 or visit our website at www.simonspeakers.com.
Jacket designed by Laura Eckes
Interior designed by Mike Rosamilia
The text of this book was set in Adobe Garamond Pro.
Manufactured in the United States of America
2 4 6 8 10 9 7 5 3 1
This book has been cataloged with the Library of Congress.
ISBN 978-1-5344-4295-5 (hc)
ISBN 978-1-5344-4297-9 (eBook)

To those who have lost,

and those who will lose.

## Row

When your older sister disappears
under the cover of night,
during a snowstorm,
leaving no tracks
and no trace,
someone should notice.

I noticed.

When she wasn't jockeying
for the shower.
When she wasn't sprawled
across the sectional
mindlessly scrolling through socials.
When she wasn't being
a total bitch.

But Ariana isn't here.

Her open bedroom door
exposes a tidy,
silent room
with a slightly rumpled duvet cover,
emanating the smell
of verbena-coconut body wash

into the hall.

I don't know where she went.
I don't know how long she's gone for,
but I'm afraid that
she might never return.

Because for the past few months
I feel like Ariana has become
that one station on the car radio
that gains more static
the farther away you drive,

like she is the one
driving farther away
from something.

But I don't know
what that something is,
and I don't know
where she is heading.

Maybe it's us.

Maybe she's driving

farther away from our history,
trying to find
her own future.

Without us.
Without me.

# Ariana

I'll tell you what grief looks like.
It's a forty-year-old woman, unshowered,
for two days, in yoga pants and a Barnard sweatshirt
and eyeliner that hasn't been scrubbed off her face.

It's dried, chapped hands that crack around the knuckles,
raw from washing away too many emotions.

It's bloated faces. It's open wine bottles.
Stained glasses that remain in the sink.

It's the nursery half-painted, half-stenciled with giraffes.
A mural unfinished. A crib disassembled on the carpet.

It's your stepmother telling your father that she's "fine."

It's my father searching for something to eat
in an empty fridge, searching for something to say.

It's me sitting at the kitchen counter
and sliding him a carton of takeout.

It's the house that was supposed to be filled
with a wailing baby, poopy diapers,
and a kid who would eventually toddle.

And it's me knowing that I should be grieving
with my family, with my father, my stepmom, and Row.

But I can't.

Because I'm trudging through the snow,
hauling an eighteen-by-twenty-four-inch
painting wrapped in brown paper
awkwardly stuck under my arm,



escaping.

# Row

Dad doesn't notice
that I slam Ariana's
bedroom door shut.

He emerges from the master bedroom
and reaches for a pot of coffee
that has turned cold
because it was
from yesterday.

I watch him microwave
the dredges
and wonder if
day-old coffee
tastes stale.

Does he notice
that Ariana isn't
standing in the kitchen
with thick droplets of water
falling to the kitchen floor
from the ends
of her waterlogged hair?

Dad returns to his bedroom
and closes the door
on the world
again.

I eat a bowl of cereal
that tastes like
living rooms,
and minivans
and family

and I look out the window
and say to no one,
"Hey, guys, it snowed."

# Ariana

I didn't just wake up at four a.m. and decide
to suddenly change my life. No one does that.
No one decides to change their life. Their life instead
changes for them. Without warning.
Without a chance to decide.

Because in the natural order of things, death is normal,
but we do a shit job at expecting it.

I'm out here due to an accumulation
of little things. For sure.
A blizzard. A blog post. A failing grade.
A general unease about living.
Like my skin doesn't know how to be
warm or cold or *normal*.

A sister.

I saw the chaos of snow flying in all directions. I heard
the rush of wind. At four in the morning, from the safety
of my bedroom window, I could see a world
that couldn't be controlled.

Finally. A picture of the world as I see it.
Outside. In the middle of a blizzard.

The thing about death is that you can never fight it.
Be it bacterial or viral,
addiction or cancer, natural causes or accidents,
something is destined to kill us.
Because in the natural order of things, dying happens.

I read a blog post on my phone, alone
in my room last night, by a girl around my age.
Her father died last summer. Cancer.
Stage four. A five-month prognosis.

I was jealous. Of all the extra time the girl
had with her father. I should know that there is
no point in playing grief Olympics. To pit one
source of pain against another.

But I find myself questioning
who had it worse?

9

What if I had a five-month warning?
How much more *Mom* could I have had?

                    Six years, thirty-seven days.

The girl admitted to the world that she thought
those last five months would be different.
She thought there would be hours of quality time.
That she and her dying father would talk about things
they never talked about. She expected to discover
new things about her father, her family, life itself.

But none of that happened.

Instead, he continued to do all the things you absolutely
do not have to do when you know you're going to die.
Go to work. Run errands. Fret about taxes.
But he did, because maybe, like me, he was scared.

To create meaning. To connect with those around you.
Because it only reminds you
of your own impending death,

and I don't want to die. Not tomorrow. Not ever.

## Row

When our mother died,
Ariana and I
didn't go to school
for a month,

even though
we were supposed to,
even though
we were just barely old enough
to spend time
alone in our house.

During that month
we learned to cook
ramen. We learned to wash
rice and crack eggs.

We never made our beds
because no one
told us to.

We spent long afternoons
lying on top
of piles of laundry.

We practiced French braids
and ponytails
and detangling
each other's hair,

and keeping secrets
and sharing secrets
and fearing the worst
and holding hands.

We stayed inside
our rambler in California,
sliding across the tile floor
in our socks,
wandering from room to room,
and sitting on the floor
of Mom's closet full of clothes
just because we could.

"Don't leave me,"
I said to Ariana
while underneath
all those clothes,

but I meant something deeper
than me. I meant
don't let it change
this feeling of us.

This frozen moment
in time when it was
just Ariana and me
and this house
and these shapeless reminders
of Mom.

Ariana held me so tight,
for so long,
that I thought
maybe we could,
we would hold on to this forever.

I know there's no longer California,
or a month without school,
or a closet full of Mom's clothes,
but I thought, Ariana,
that we still had us,


to hold on to, forever.

## Ariana

Pellets of snow and ice smack me in the face
and the wind blows from every angle.

The butcher paper tears at the corners,
and the canvas underneath begins to poke through.

The package slides out from under my armpit.
I stop and readjust. Shift the painting to my other arm.

Maybe I should have put the whole thing
in a giant trash bag
and hauled it over my shoulder.
It's not like it's heavy.

It's not like it should be hard to carry a painting
in the wind,
protecting it from the snow, trying not to drop it
while walking
to the bus station in a snowstorm.

What would people say about what I am doing?
Would they call it selfish? Desperate? Ill-advised.

A car fishtails at the stoplight ahead. The back wheels
begin to skid, but the driver regains control
and straightens onto the dark street ahead.

It's way too snowy and way too early for either of us
to be out here on the streets heading somewhere.
But we are.

Because, like snowstorms and earthquakes and death,
your future will happen regardless of whether
you planned for it.

# Row

I walked through the door
after practice
on Thursday.

My family stood
in the living room
staring down
at what looked like
a porcelain crime scene.

"That was your mother's favorite."
Dad's hands trembled
as he got down
and picked broken pieces
off the floor.

I tossed aside shin guards
and stripped off socks.
"What's going on?"
But no one answered.

"Row, I have something
to tell you,"
Maribel started.

She winced
and doubled over.

I froze.

Dad sprang to his feet.
He cooed into Maribel's ear
and rubbed her back
with such vigor
that the cotton tunic
she wore began to bunch.

I felt the sting
of sliding on artificial turf
run all over my skin.

Ariana just stared
at the pile on the floor.

"Why can't we have
something good for once?"

"Ariana," Dad said.
"Please don't make it worse."

My sister was
a tangled knot of hair,
the kind you need
scissors to cut out.

"God. The cramps,"
Maribel said,
gritting her teeth,
clutching her side.

The room was large and exposed.
All the lights were on.
I heard them buzzing.

Ariana didn't even flinch.

I should have
said something to Maribel.
I should have
said something to Ariana.
Put her in check.

But it's like I couldn't.

Because Ariana was
sucking all of the courage

and strength
out of the room.
She consumed everything
that might have helped
just by standing there
doing nothing.

The words I might have said.
To Maribel. To let her know
that we were here for her.
We saw her pain.

But I didn't do anything
because all I could focus on
was my older sister and her
selfish, self-involved pain.

Dad led Maribel
back into the bedroom.
I heard the door close
with a distant click.

"What happened?" I said.

"Nothing," said Ariana.
She gritted her teeth

and clenched her jaw,
just like Maribel,
trying to fight away pain.

"What happened?" I repeated,
still holding my soccer bag.
Feeling the weight
of the gear on my shoulder.

"I threw one of Mom's figurines."

"What happened?"
I said again, firmly this time.
Ariana still didn't respond,
but I didn't need her to tell me
anything about what was going on.

I felt it, like the dread
of picking up
an unexpected phone call,
knowing what the person
on the other end
was going to say
but wanting them
to say it anyway.
To make it real.

"It's the baby, isn't it?" I said.

Ariana held the broken shards
of a porcelain in her palm.
She closed her hand around it,
and I wondered
if she did this
just to feel
the sharp edges
of pain piercing,
but not breaking, the skin.

We stood there
in front of the couch
where just yesterday
we marathoned a show
about small-town secrets
and portals to another world.

Now it's like I've entered the portal
and found a different sister.

If she were a player on my team,
I'd find the words
to give her a pep talk,
reinforce the strengths
she possesses,

point out a weakness
on the other side's defense,
and show her a way
to break through.

But recently, I'm not sure
she's even on my same team.

Or if instead she's simply
walked off the field,

because that's what it feels like

not a teammate
or an opponent,

but a sister
who refuses
to play.

# Row

"It's not a competition," I said.
"You don't get to be the only one
who feels it. You don't get to consume
all the sadness in the world."

"Feels what?"
Ariana finally looked up.

"The steaming pile of shit
that is grief."

"What do you want me
to say, Row?"

Ariana looked the same
as always in a lot of ways.
Like her round cheeks
were still holding on
to being a child,
the way that my body
did the same,

but there was something else
that I hadn't really noticed.

If you looked at her
long enough,
her rounded face
would begin to fall,
the muscles strained
to a point where they decided
to give up.

I always thought that as sisters
we would be unchanging.
I thought that was the whole point.

That sisters were like baby blankets.
With you since the crib,
and even though colors may fade
and stitching unravels,
we would still hold
that same smell
of being a kid.

I guess I thought
that even as Ariana and I
grew older, grew bigger,
we didn't have to change
for each other.

But that wasn't happening.

Ariana was growing
each day
into a person
I didn't know.

I love my sister, but

I wanted to feel
proud and inspired.
I wanted to share her
with everyone and no one.

But the Ariana
who was crouched on the floor
picking up shards
of a broken figurine
was someone I didn't like,

someone with a cold, unfeeling heart,
a bristled soul layered in ice.

I didn't know what she could say
to make it better,

because it wasn't words
that I wanted.

It was action.

"What is wrong with you?
You're better than this."

# Ariana

Even there in the bus station I can't escape from it.
The reminders of death. A song is playing.
Alex's song. The one about ghosts.

This song is following me, I swear. The way a refrain
gets stuck in your head and follows you
from room to room,
moment to moment,
maybe days on end.

Until it eventually fades.

"Your student ID," a woman at the ticket counter
with a haggard face interrupts.

I am struck by the normalness of it all.

It's just like the first time we all went to the grocery store
after Mom died to get milk and eggs and stuff.
The whole time, all I could think about was
that our mom had died
and nobody in there knew.

Nobody knew that this was our new normal.

I was surprised how easy
it was to exist as a faceless child.
A person that no one knew anything about.
But I remember having this feeling
that I *wanted* people to know.

*I am the girl with the dead mother.*

Standing in front of the ticket counter at the bus station,
it's like that first time all over again.
When the woman behind the counter asks me again
for my student ID, I have this impulse
that I want her to know.

*I am the girl with the dead mother.*

I set the painting on the linoleum floor.
I unzip every pocket but can't find my ID.

"Just give me an adult ticket," I say.
I'm trying to be someone more.

The woman nods. "Bus boards in twenty minutes."

# Row

I stare into the empty living room
at a quiet couch, a lonely blanket,
and remember the time
a bird flew into this room.

Small with yellow and red feathers.
It flapped its wings frantically
and bounced from wall to wall.

Ariana and I were alone
with the bird.

"You left the door open,"
she said.

"For two seconds. I swear."
I shut the door.

The bird flew smack
into a window and continued
to flap around, scared
like we were.

"What are you doing?
Open it back up!"

The bird pooped on a bookcase.

A white smear slid down
the wooden exterior.
A small splatter
hit the spine
of a book.

"A bird poops
every ten minutes,"
I said, as if it were
our call to action.

Ten minutes until
it poops again,
until Dad comes home,
until the bird flies
into something breakable.

Framed family photos.
Mom's collection of figurines.

"I saw this in a movie," Ariana said.
She handed me a corner of a blanket.

"What movie?"

"Does it matter?"

We unfurled the blanket like a flag
and held both ends
across the room,
trying to sweep the bird,
coax it closer to the door.

At first it just flew over us,
avoiding the blanket entirely.

But then, maybe it knew
that this strange environment
it landed in wasn't home.

Maybe it missed
the trees and the wind
and the other birds.

Maybe it started to feel caged
flying from wall to wall.
Hitting the windows,
perching on things
that weren't green.

The bird flew without coaxing
straight out the door,
heading for the woods,
like it was all a temporary detour
in bird life to see what it might be like
to live in a house
with the two of us.

Ariana collapsed
on the couch
with the blanket.

I plucked a book off the shelf.

"What do you think it says
that the bird chose
to poop on *Little Women*?" I said.

"It's still pissed that Amy
ends up with Laurie," Ariana replied.

I wiped the bird poop off with my sleeve.
Ariana blinked hard at me. She shook her head.
"Gotta love a sister who will wipe up literal shit."

I shrugged and curled up next to her
on the couch, together reading
the first page, silently
holding our breath, wondering
what it would be like

if someone were to tell a story,
not of four little
white girls from New England,

but of brown girls,
who loved each other fiercely
and of a world
that didn't get
in their way.

## Ariana

Our mother came from an island where it never snowed.
She would have hated this.
"This isn't natural," she would have said.

She came from an island where families are traced
through their mothers, grandmothers, aunties, and
great-aunties.

On our mother's island, women inherited the land.
Women had a final say in governance.
Women defined and shaped and perpetuated the culture.

So when the colonizers came, they were baffled.
What are we supposed to do with an island governed
by *women*?

In the wars against the colonialists, women survived.
Women held on with power and land and culture in
their fists.

I wonder how our mother would have raised us
as young women. I wonder what she could have taught us
about governance and power, about running a household,
a community, a culture. I think about who she was
before she died. The breadwinner with a fancy corporate job.

Maybe she was trying to show us culture,
through her place in the household with Dad.

But there's one other thing that women
from the island are supposed to do.
Mothers are supposed to determine
the destiny of their own children.
The place and role children will assume in the future.

But when your mother dies, what happens
to your own destiny?
Who are you supposed to be?
What role are you to assume
if your mother isn't there to guide you?

# Row

I text my sister
wherever she is.

There's a lot of fricken snow outside.

For ten, then twenty,
then thirty seconds,
Ariana doesn't respond.

Maybe it's because I didn't
ask her a question.

I text her again.
Why aren't you here?

I really expect her to respond.
I don't even care what she says.
Just to know that she's out there
thinking of me.

We've been through a lot of crap.
I get it. But I'm still here.
I'm your sister.

The screen starts to dim
like a slow goodbye,
the kind where someone says,
Hey, I'm going now,
before they finally leave.

I want to believe
that she's going to text back,
but there's nothing.

While everyone else
is watching their mothers
soar over them like an airplane,
skirting around weather formations,
showing them different routes,

all I have is Ariana,
who doesn't know how to fly.

I watch my sister approach her future
with the reluctance
of a train conductor,
and while everyone else
is flying around in airplanes,
who is left to use the rails?

It's me, Ariana.
I'm behind you.
Stuck on this line,
pulled along the same
steel tracks as you.

But if you're not here, ahead of me,
who am I to follow?
How am I supposed to learn?

# Ariana

"I don't know what to do with you Ariana,"
Ms. Wex said as she sat at her desk, flipping through
a grade book after class a week ago.

"Because you're technically failing this class.
You were supposed to complete a portfolio,
tied together with a single theme.
Like Rory's over there."

Ms. Wex paused, searching for something
more to say about Rory's work.

"Her theme is supposed to be letters. Like the alphabet,"
I said. I nodded at a cubist-style painting
of an apple and a surrealist take on a boat.

There was a technical quality to each image,
but nothing that screamed out with heart.

"Five original works of art," Ms. Wex continued.
"That's what I wrote on the syllabus. You have
produced only one. And the theme?"

Ms. Wex looked at my painting again. Her head tilted,
in the kind of way that said, *I don't really know where my eyes
are supposed to look, and the color is all confusing.*

"Grief," I said. "It's about grief."

"Okaaay," Ms. Wex said, but it came out long and drawn out
and affectless, like she could have been saying
any other word, like "potato" or "suitcase" or "carrot."

"The school counselor tells me you need
this class to graduate, so I'm giving you a chance
to improve your grade. You won't get an A,
but at least you won't fail."

"I might not graduate?" A lump grew in my throat.
One that felt like it had been growing
since the beginning of senior year,
whenever I thought about things
related to my future.

Ms. Wex didn't look up or nod or acknowledge my question.
She scribbled on a pad of paper. Her handwriting,
exacting. Each letter angled and pointed.

"There's a gallery show in the city next Saturday.
A special exhibit for high school students.

I'm offering extra credit for those
who choose to participate.

Part of being an artist is learning
how to let your work speak for itself on display."

I didn't know I was failing or that I was
at risk to not graduate. I figured I still had time
to produce more. Anything. To retake the class.

How could I have been so careless to think
that there would be more time?
I should have known better.
There is never enough time.

Ms. Wex slid across a piece of paper
with a date, a time, and an address.

I looked at my lonely painting on the easel.
A frayed edge of canvas.

It looked exactly the way I intended,

even though it took me this entire semester
just to get over the fear of making
this painting, that I didn't have to
let go of the grief; I just had to let it all out.

I watched Ms. Wex's eyes drift over to my painting,
then dart back to mine. Like she was afraid of it.
Of what it might mean and say.

Part of me wanted to take the painting
and shove it in a closet forever,

but I folded up the piece of paper
into a stubby little square
and pocketed it in my bag.

because maybe if I did hang it up on a wall,
maybe if Ms. Wex, if I, if all of us,
stared at the painting long enough,

we would stop being so afraid.

# Row

I know I shouldn't put
this much weight
on a single text.

But I do.

Because every second
Ariana fails to answer

I worry about
who we have
become.

I want us to be something
that resembles a family.

Like a soccer team,
all running around a field
in choreographed patterns,
heading toward the same goal.

But that's not what our family is.

It's a frayed string of lights
that someone needs to fix
with electrical tape.

It's the electricity
that can't get to us
because Mom's bulb
has burned out,
so now the whole string is dark.

But without the lights turned on,
does anyone even notice
that we are broken?

# Ariana

The overhead storage is too narrow for my painting.
The floor space too dirty. The seat next to me,
not wide enough. I settle on resting the painting
on my knees and lean it against the seat back in front of me.

Air is blasting through tiny vents overhead,
smelling like strangers. A guy in front of me
eats a bag of chips, an elderly woman
hugs a reusable bag. Her eyes dart around.

Her shoulders fold inward. She hugs
the bag tighter as people pass her by,
like she's afraid of something.

Is it the snowstorm brewing outside?
The safety record of the driver?
Is it the place that she's headed
or what she's leaving behind?

Or is she just afraid of the rest of us
trying to steal all her stuff?

Sometimes I wonder what people think about.
Whether their feelings are intense, like mine,
or completely ordinary and mundane.

Sometimes I wonder what it might be like
to spend a whole day thinking about small,
insignificant things. Like the scratchiness
of the seat fabric or the steady breeze of recycled air.

The driver releases the brake, the bus rolls forward.

I take a few breaths, sink down into the upholstered seats,
trying to feel excited that I'm here,
doing something, anything,
not just for a passing grade,

but to convince myself that I don't have to be so scared
of the future. I don't have to be scared of the past.

# Row

I stare at the screen, rereading
the unanswered text.

I think back to the first month of school.
When the captain of the soccer team
called out to me
in the hall.

She stood in the center
of a circle of senior girls
talking with confidence
about weekends and parties and classes.

I shifted my weight
from one leg to the other.
Tucked the short ends
of hair behind my ear.

"Great game last night, Twenty-four."

"Uh-huh," I said,
but I wasn't really
paying attention.

I spotted Ariana.
Her thick and loose ponytail.
The yellow cardigan
that matched a pair of sneakers
I had in my closet.
I saw a girl who looked like me,
but wasn't me.

I watched Ariana
duck around the corner
as soon as I caught her eye.

She saw me.
But it's like here in high school
she didn't even know me.

The senior girls were staring.
"That's your sister?"
one of them said,
the blond one
people called "Busy"

and I never really knew
whether it was
a given name,
a nickname,
or a reputation.

"Yeah," I said.

"Huh. I don't recognize her,"
the one named Rory said.
The captain nudged her.
"She's in our English class."

"Really?"

"Isn't she friends with that girl
from that band? You know, the band
that actually ended up making it,"
Busy said.

They all tilted their heads
peering into the vacated space
that Ariana once occupied,
then back at me.

Sometimes it's like
Ariana disappeared
altogether.

I run into
my best friend, Kennedy,
without even trying.

I see half the team
every time I use the bathroom.

But I could go days on end
without seeing Ariana anywhere.

"But she's so quiet," said Rory.

I tilted my head and tried to see
Ariana the way her classmates saw her.

But I couldn't.

She wasn't a mystery, or a rumor,
or a quiet girl who sat in the back of class.
She was my sister, and that's all I could see
in the vacated space.

A shadow once occupied by my sister.

# Ariana

I glance down at the phone in my hand.
There's a text from Row lighting up the screen.
What if she wants me to be sisterly and strong?

When Row scored the winning goal in the state finals,
Dad's face literally glowed, like he was so happy and so proud
he didn't know whether to cry or to scream.
Instead he reached out to me, to Maribel,
and pulled us in close. I wanted to feel happy
along with them, but the muscles that held my smile ached.

What would they say if they knew I was failing
because I couldn't get my act together?
I lost track of time. I was supposed to
graduate and go on and be normal. Like Row.

I didn't feel like anyone's older sister. Not right now.
Maybe I could go to the art show. Get my passing grade.
Return home and then I would pull out the catalogs
of college choices. I would ask Row and Maribel for help.

We would sit down together
and pore over pictures
and no one would remember the day it snowed,

when I failed to leave a note, respond to a text.
When I disappeared for hours

because I was scared of them finding out
that I wasn't well adjusted.
I wasn't normal.
I wasn't strong and sisterly.

I'm just me.

The light is starting to break through the trees.
The snow has stopped,
but the thick white clouds hover off in the distance.
The countryside disappears
at sixty miles an hour, and I lean my head
against a window with finger smudges
and nose prints, slipping the phone back into my pocket,
turning the ringer to silent.

# Row

The baby must have passed away
just hours after Maribel returned home
from her doctor's appointment
where our sister was said to be
a healthy weight and size.

Our sister's heart stopped beating,
like our mother's, unexpectedly,
on a day that was otherwise
normal.

I wonder what it was like for Maribel
to hold on to something
that had died.

I wish that I could see Maribel
to know that she will be okay,

even after the cramping passes,
the bleeding stops,
after our sister is exhumed
from her body.

I look over at the closed master bedroom
and hear nothing.

No television. No voices.
No crying. No shower.

I look down the hall at Ariana's door.
The silence without her is deafening.

I go to my room, close the door,
and turn on a podcast about soccer
just to fill the room with noise.

But I wish it wasn't just talking.
I wish there was someone around
who could listen.

# Row

I remember our first snowfall together. Here

in my room Ariana and I watched

the way that snow tries to

seclude us as neighbors'

houses disappeared

among snow

drifts.

"I miss
her," Ariana
said after twenty
minutes of soundless
gazing. I remember her
voice, the way it trembled
with uncertainty. I remember
the thick salty tears that welled
in my eyes and when Ariana brushed
her hand against my shoulder, I couldn't
hold them back. Neither could she. Neither
could the sky that dumped clumps of snow. I
remember looking out at the landscape and back at
Ariana, seeing the extent to which people can change
so quickly. The way flakes could pile up one speck at a
time and transform the world before us into shapeless mounds.
I remember the feeling of us, together, letting ourselves cry over snow.

# Ariana

We're supposed to have a backstory.
We're supposed to have a series of life experiences
that have brought us to this moment in time.

I'm sitting on a bus that's headed away
from the place where I live, because I'm failing
art class, jeopardizing whatever future I'm supposed
to be having, and not even questioning how the hell I got here.

I'm just here. The product of a failed backstory.

In German there is a word for experience, *Erlebnis*,
which comes from the verb *erleben*,
and translates as *living through something*.

In English, we have no succinct word
for living through something.

Maybe it could have been different had I not been there
watching my mom fall to the floor at a Starbucks,
dropping her phone and clawing at her chest.

The newspaper she held fluttered to the floor,
the way a heart might sometimes flutter.
Not because you're nervous or falling in love.

But like when you're sitting at your desk
in the middle of a trigonometry test
and your heart unexpectedly flutters.

I remember the wail of the steamer frothing milk.
The barista on her cell phone. The paramedics
scurrying around my mother. I remember I stood there
in silence, frozen against an immovable display case full of crap.
Like maybe if I stayed real still, time itself would slow down.

But time didn't stop. The world didn't slow down
with me. It kept on plowing ahead.

In the aftermath of death, those of us who survive
have little preparation for what we're actually supposed to do
with our lives from that point forward.

Like the entire concept of having a backstory is erased.
There is only before your mother died, and now.

Each day is now.

It feels neither farther nor closer to the moment she died.
It feels like another day, of actions and reactions,
but without anything to live through, without *Erlebnis*.

# Row

I text all seventeen girls
from the varsity squad
to see if anyone is down
for a pickup game of soccer,
because when I'm on a field
people listen to me.
They pay attention.

My teammates. They see me.
My opponents. They see me.
The people in the stands.
Coaches. Scouts.
I am a player to be seen.

I know it's not the right kind of listening
or the right kind of being seen.
But being noticed, even if it's not
for the thing that you want to be noticed for,
still feels all right, like you matter
and there is someone out there who cares.

I'm not saying that Dad
and Ariana don't care.
It's just sometimes I think they forget
how to listen

because after Mom died it was hard
to hear anything other than silence.

# Row

The snow is a real killjoy.

Absolutely no one
wants to leave their crackling fire
or the warm cup of cocoa
or the raucous game of Monopoly
they've entered into with their siblings
to lace up their cleats
and tromp through the snow
for a pickup game of soccer.

Seriously, you'll be fine.
You're definitely going to make
the premier team.

Just take a day off
for once.

You're obsessed, 24.

Twenty-four.

My number. My identity.

It's what I've led them all to believe.

I am Twenty-four.
Not Row.
Not Ariana's little sister.
Not a girl without a mother.

I'm a number.
A position.
A series of county
and state records.

And I've done nothing to correct them
because a large part of me wants to believe
that this is who I am.

A seriously talented,
seriously obsessed
soccer player
who is singularly focused
on the game,
on the win.

Except,
with Ariana gone
I know that's not true,
not even close.

I am a person
who is scared,
who is empty,
and who is alone

without her family.

# Ariana

*You were robbed* were the words
a classmate once told me in eighth grade.

We flipped through magazines her mother
still subscribed to. Mostly about home decor
and living your best life. We scrolled through our phones
looking at photos of people we didn't know,
and then she asked me what my mom did "for a living."

"Nothing. She died."

That's when she told me I was robbed. Like I hadn't noticed.
Like anyone who is robbed wouldn't notice that their purse
was yanked off their shoulder or that there's broken glass
by the back door and the flat-screen is missing.

It wasn't helpful to be reminded of this.
Robbed of all the things my mother
was supposed to teach me.

I could learn from the internet the difference
between menstrual cups, tampons, and pads.
I could learn from a Google search home remedies
on how to relieve cramps, and my questions about sex?
There were plenty of sources for that.

But what the internet lacked were any real lessons
on how to navigate this world as a young woman
who felt solely defined by her grief.

My classmate changed the subject to whether or not
I thought we were too young to date high schoolers.

"You should ask your mother," I told her.
She shifted her body. Raised the magazine to her face,
and never invited me back to her house.

My grief makes people uncomfortable.
It reminds even adults that we're all going to die.
That bad things really do happen to good people.

I am not a walking disease because my mother died.
I am not abnormal. I am not contagious.

I am a human with grief. Just like we all will be someday.
Because there is only one universal truth in this world.

That we and everyone around us will someday die,
and grief is all that remains in the aftermath.

# Row

Snow,
I text Kennedy,

one of those friends
who is always down
for doing something.
Except soccer.

Because, as Kennedy puts it,
"My two left feet wouldn't know
how to run down a field,
let alone kick a ball straight."

"It's not that hard,"
I've told her.

"It is for someone who has
no desire to play in the first place,"
she would always say in response.

Of course I know it snowed.
This house has windows.
They are used to see out into the world,
and sometimes reflections
of ourselves,

Kennedy writes back.

Deep,
I text.

She sends over a photo
of snow
through a window
with a faint reflection
of Kennedy
snapping a photo
of snow
through a window.

Meta, I respond.

But seriously.
I stopped by on Thursday
and the lights were on
but no one answered the door.
What's going on over there?
Kennedy writes.

I thought about
writing something

meaningful,
maybe vulnerable.
People were real into
talking about being vulnerable.
I thought about sharing.

And then I send
an emoji
of a pineapple
and a snowman
and an upside-down
smiley face.

Friendships are like plants.
They require care and watering,
Kennedy responds.

I snap a photo
of the houseplant
named Earl.
Friends.

I know your stepmother
waters that, not you.

# Ariana

Snow blankets the low, flat ground
where underneath maybe there is land
to sow seeds in or fields to play on.

Maybe it's land where kids play baseball
or soccer or get lost in a corn maze.

I wonder if my sister is just now waking up,
if she's looking out her window and contemplating
what clothes she could wear in order to still
play soccer in all this snow. Like there's nothing
in her life that will stop her from getting out there on the field.

I want that depth of determination. I want to feel
like nothing can get in my way. I want to chase after something
the way Row chases after the ball.

I remember watching the way younger girls
follow my sister on the field with their eyes.

The way they'd startle and then cheer when Row
cuts a ball left and taps one, then two
into the goal.

I remember seeing their tiny hands gripping the fence
during the semifinals, noses peering through,
and wondering if they realized that this wasn't normal.

People didn't show up to watch soccer.
People didn't show up to watch
high school women play anything.

But during the semifinals, the stands were packed.

I overheard the owner of the diner on Main Street
seated on the bleacher in front of me explain
to the owner of the hardware store about offsides.

A group of senior guys had brought cardboard cutouts
of players' faces. My sister's head bobbled around.

Out of the woodwork, everyone who ever wanted to feel
like they could be worthy of something
showed up to the games.

Because we all wanted to see for ourselves
what it could be like to be so good at something
that other people noticed.

Maribel and Dad showed up looking flustered.
The half was just about to end.

"I can't believe we're late. The appointment ran over."
Maribel rubbed her belly, the small
noticeable bump starting to show.

She leaned over to me as we watched the team
jog off the field and huddle around the coach.

"It's a girl," Maribel leaned over and said.

It was this type of world that I wanted a sister to grow up in.
One that could celebrate her accomplishments
not because she was a girl but because she was worthy.

But I wasn't the one on the field.
I wasn't the one with the cardboard cutout of my face.
I wasn't doing anything to create a type of future
that I wanted for a future sister,

because I wasn't doing anything
to create a type of future that I wanted for myself.

I had no clue what to do.

A whistle blew and the second half started.
I watched the game descend into a slog of possession.
The crowd was rapt with every play.
Every corner. Every turnover.

I watched Row go after the ball.

Targeting a player. Legs pounding against the field,
and I saw something that I didn't know how to have.

But even there, surrounded by hundreds of people,
all chanting Row's name, I couldn't help
but drift away and think about Mom.
How she would be so proud of Row.

She would have loved to be here, to see someone just like her.
Someone who could attack life the way she did.

But what would she say about me?

The daughter in the stands who doesn't
have any real hobbies or talents to speak of.

The daughter who is supposed to grow up and be something
but has no idea what that something is
or how to find it and pursue it

the way that Row pursues a player.

The daughter who can't seem to let go of her mother.
The daughter who still wishes that she could be held forever.

## Row

Ten minutes later
Kennedy texts again.

Do you want
to build a
snowmaaaan?

I am not
your Elsa,
I text back.

Well, then,
ask your sister.

# Row

I type and delete
and type again
and let the words
sit on the screen
like turtles on a log
sunning themselves
in springtime.

Ariana's not here.

## Ariana

I once saw Row talking to Rory from Studio Art;
Busy, the girl who invited me to her house in seventh grade,
the girl with the magazines and a friendship I thought
that maybe I could have had; and Paola,
the girl that everyone thought was Row's older sister,

because they're both brown and play soccer,
and except for the whole different-parents,
different-last-name thing, people still assume that they are.

Row and I haven't been at the same school together
since California. Since before Mom died.

We haven't had to occupy the same halls,
interact with the same people.

Row hasn't had to see me, in my world,
and now she was here, and it was her world.

It was like suddenly my sister was different.
Not my little sister. But one of them.

One of the normal, well-adjusted girls
who could walk down the hall
every day and talk to people.

One of the girls who had a lunch table to sit at,
friends who texted her, a whole team of people
who called out her number down the hall.

I didn't recognize her.
I didn't recognize myself.

It was senior year and I didn't even have
a regular table to sit at in the cafeteria.

Like all the years before I snuck bites of food
in the library during lunch while doing homework,
and for all these years it has been fine. I even liked it.

But I watched Row talk to Busy, Rory, and Paola.

I didn't want her to know that after all these years
I hadn't moved on. I hadn't found my place
in this world like she had. I hadn't figured out
who I was, and it scared me. Because someday
I needed to leave, and what was I supposed to do
with an entire future?

What would Row say if she found out
I wasn't a good model to follow? I wasn't

a sister who would pave the way. That she
didn't have a mother or an older sister around to guide her.

I didn't want her to see me, so

I slipped around the corner and disappeared.

# Row

Why would anyone
go outside in this weather?
Kennedy texts back.

There's, like, seven inches of snow
and it's fifteen degrees out at best.

I look out the window again
and see ice crystals swirl into snowdrifts.
*Where is she?*

I try to push aside the feeling
of being left behind.

So, you wanna come over here?
I text. I feel a small pang of guilt
immediately after pushing send.
Like I'm trying to replace
Ariana with Kennedy.

I don't know.
Maybe I am.
Maybe I should.

You heard me, right?
Why on earth would I want
to trudge through this weather
and hang out at your house?

Because we're friends.
Then I drop in an emoji
of two girls dancing.

# Ariana

The bus stops at the next station an hour later.
A kid about eight sits down next to me, while his mother
and baby sister take empty seats a few rows forward.

"I'm Edward," the kid says, unprompted,
pulling out a stack of books.
Volumes about animals. "What's your favorite animal?"

I don't answer. I try to tune him out by pulling down
my knit hat and resting my head against the window.

But he keeps talking, and asks me again,
"What's your favorite animal?"

"A jellyfish," I finally answer, because
when I think about jellyfish, I think about silence.

"Whoa. That's cool." Edward flips
to a page in his animal encyclopedia.

"Did you know that there are certain
kinds of jellyfish that can live forever?"
He starts to read an entry.

*"'Once the immortal jellyfish reaches adulthood,*
*it transforms back into its original juvenile state.'"*

"I hate to break it to you, kid,
but nothing lives forever."

# Row

Kennedy stands inside our front door
twenty minutes later,
unraveling the layers
of clothes wrapped around her.

The snow on Kennedy's boots
begins melting
on the tile floor,
yet I still feel cold
standing here
in wool socks.

"For real. It's a blizzard out there,
and my mom is less than thrilled
about me leaving the house,
but I said that I was worried
about you guys."

She's looking around the kitchen
and starting to notice that no one
has turned on any lights
this morning.

She notices
the recycle bin overflowing
with milk cartons
and yogurt containers
that no one has touched
in three days.

"Um. No offense,"
Kennedy begins,
"but it feels a little
like a cesspool
of sadness in here,
and something is
literally rotting."

It's like she can see
all of our emotions
out on display.

I don't want to
have to explain to her
right now what's going on.

I don't want to share
with her about Maribel,
or the baby, or about how it feels
when grief seeps back
under your skin,
like a roof that leaks
one drop at a time.

Instead, I wish I just had
the foresight to clean.

# Ariana

The bus rumbles into the college town of Loganville,
and there's a line of students clutching to-go cups
and overnight bags for the city.

In the distance, grounds crews with snow shovels
and vehicles outfitted with plows scrape away
ice and snow on tree-lined walkways in front of red brick dorms.

This is exactly how college looks in the glossy catalogs
that Maribel had sent to our house. I get it.

It's like the perfect interlude in a song. Like sun breaks
after a long spell of rain. Like the day after it snows,
and even though it's freezing, you wouldn't trade anything
for the way the world glistens, untouched.

But it's like I have an aversion to this level of a stylized future.
Everyone with their Bean boots and quilted totes.

"I think you'll be surprised to find people
who you relate to," Maribel once said to me.

She held out a stack of brochures.
"They may have different life experiences,
but there's something about lying around a dorm room
and bonding, the collective hardship of challenging classes,
the shared yearning to be someone better," she said.

How can it be better? How can it be so perfect?
The experiences of our lives cannot be reversed.

"It's not about the best school. Private or public.
In state or out of state. Two-year or four-year.
It's about who you show up as
during your college experience."

A girl stands alone, waiting to board. Checking her phone.

In the distance, across the quad, I see a group of brown girls
in sweatpants and bundled in oversize jackets.
Laughing. I wonder what is so funny. I wonder
what it feels like to laugh so hard that your breath
looks like clouds coming out of your mouth.

I want to believe Maribel, because maybe she is right.
Because she at least knows what it's like. She's Filipina,
like Dad. She's brown, like us. She knows what it means
to be and have been a young brown woman,
to exist in our skin.

She knows how to believe in a future.
She knows how to make one.

I want to believe, because Mom isn't here,
and Maribel is trying.

# Row

"Are you going to help?"
Kennedy empties
an overflowing recycle bin.

I follow her into the garage,
where she dumps the contents
into a large blue canister.

Someone,
someday,
will have to haul
the recycle bin
out to the street.

Preferably after
someone,
someday,
shovels the driveway,
but I didn't want it to be me,
the only member of this household
who is around to notice
the chores to be done.

Besides, Dad was the one
who loved shoveling snow.

It must be an adult thing.

The satisfaction
of clearing the way
for the inhabitants
of a home.
Of providing something
as small as a pathway
out to the rest of the world.

Excavating trenches
in a battle against
Mother Nature.

Except for the imprints
left behind
by Kennedy's snow boots,
no one has cleared a pathway
to the street.

No one scraped the driveway bare.
No one has ventured outside
since the snow started falling,

except my sister

who left at some point

in the middle of the night

when the snow fell the hardest

and her longing to escape

overwhelmed her.

# Ariana

A girl with a guitar case strapped to her back runs for the bus.
Someone is trailing behind. I hunker down low in my seat.
But as soon as she enters the bus, she sees me.

"Ariana?" She stops a few rows ahead of me,
holding up a line of passengers behind.

"Hey. Alex." Of course. After all these months.
Alex gets on my bus. After all these months
of trying to forget her.

Alex looks a little flustered too. Like she's not quite sure
she wants to see me either, but someone brushes her bag.
She glances over her shoulder and points to the girl behind her.

"This is my roommate," Alex says.

Her roommate looks normal. The way a well-adjusted
college girl might look. Clothes draped over her body
in effortless layers. Skin that is hydrated and blemish free.
She probably uses toner. She probably knows why
one is supposed to use toner.

"We should grab those seats," the roommate says,
pointing to the remaining pair toward the back.

There are so many things to say to Alex.
Even the small things like, how are you?
How's the band? How's college and life and your future?

Maybe she wants me to ask her one of those questions.
Any question. Because she lingers a moment longer.
"Okay, sure. It was good seeing you, Ariana."

The bus shifts into gear. Alex wavers down the aisle, and I watch
as she finds her seat and pulls a muffin out from a jacket pocket
and starts eating, spilling crumbs onto the floor.

# Row

"So, is Ariana just gone?
Or like *Gone Girl* gone?"
Kennedy asks.

"What do you mean?"

"Should I be worried?"
Kennedy says, but she's already worried.
I don't know why people always think
that worrying will resolve anything.

Like when Mom died,
our parents' friends
were always like,

"We are so worried about you girls."

Ariana would respond,
"What good does that do?
She's not coming back."

That always shut people up.

"Something's not right, Row."

We're usually so good
at looking normal. The food
in the fridge is where it should be.
The plates put away. The blankets strewn
across the couch because we use them.

"I'm kinda concerned about you guys,"
Kennedy continues,
her eyes darting around.

"Like, where is your sister?"

"I don't know," I say.

"Aren't you even remotely concerned?"

My legs feel antsy.
I thought Kennedy would
come over and we would
chill and hang out,
and not really think
about what might be
going on in this family.

There's a whole season
of quality escapism
we could be watching.

Or maybe a board game?
When was the last time
we did that?

Or maybe I should have opted
for soccer. Maybe playing alone
would have been better than

Kennedy here in this house
interrogating the inner workings
of our family.

We're not okay. I get it.
But does it need to be
on display for anyone else?

"Like, what if
she's in a snowy ditch
on the side of the road,
unconscious
and freezing to death?

"Or, like, what if something really
bad happened, like that girl
who was discovered in the woods?
You know, murdered."

"Jesus, Kennedy."

"That was a really terrible thing
for me to say. I'm sure she's not dead."

My face must be saying something
that my mouth can't,
because Kennedy's cheeks
turn three shades redder.

"I. Am. So. Sorry," she says
with a deliberateness
that people reserve
for speaking in public,
but there's no one else around
to hear her words.

Just me.

I shake my head.

It's not out of the realm
of possibility. Bad things.
Horrible, unspeakable things
happen all the time
to good people.
The worst-case scenario.

You would think that a person
would have a quota
on the number
of worst-case scenarios
that happen in one's life.

But they just keep happening.

"She's only gone," I say.

Not missing. Left.

I can tell by the shoes
that Ariana took with her.
The bag that is gone.
The snacks that are now empty,
which she must have packed.

But I don't know the depth
to which she's missing
from us.

# Row

"Well, if Ariana,
a perfectly normal human being
living and breathing in this world,
is not here at this present moment,
then where do you think she went?"

I watch Kennedy open the fridge,
helping herself to the last seltzer water.
I'm slightly annoyed.

Because Kennedy gets to
navigate this house
with such ease,
because this isn't actually
her family,
or her problem,
or her sister
who is gone.

She's just here to hang out,
and I wish I could be a person
who could hang out too,

instead of pretending to be chill
while keeping it all together.

I miss Ariana.
I miss the baby, too.

I want to tell Ariana
that it's going to be okay,
we still have us,

but I think about how we both
wanted *us* to mean three.

"What if we Nancy Drew this situation?"
Kennedy says. The carbonation
in her can sizzles.

"What do you mean?"

She exits the kitchen,
and I follow her
to Ariana's closed
bedroom door.

So many closed doors.

"Well, according to
my extensive knowledge

watching prime-time procedurals,
maybe we should search for clues."

I know there's nothing to be found
in Ariana's room, because
whatever mysteries
Ariana harbors,
she carries with her
in her heart.

Somewhere away.

But I nod. "Um. Okay."
Because even if she comes back
today, tonight, or tomorrow,

maybe I can find something
that will remind us both
of the sisters
we are meant
to be.

# Ariana

"Who? Was? That?" my seatmate, Edward, asks.

"An old friend," I say.

Edward turns around in his seat. "She looks like a rock star."
Even without the guitar, he must be reacting to the way
her face looks perpetually badass. The way her hoodie
hangs from her shoulders, like even her clothes don't give a shit.

"She's in a band," I say.

"You're her friend?" Edward peeks his head around
to catch another glimpse of Alex.

"Not anymore."

"Why not?" He turns back to me.

I shake my head. "It's complicated."

"Because she got too famous," Edward says definitively.

"It's not that."

"Did you get in a fight?" Edward says.

I wish I could pinpoint something big and dramatic
that happened, something that people would be able
to react to and say, *Yeah, I get it.*

But it wasn't like that.
How could I tell people that I
didn't want to be her friend,
that I didn't see myself in our friendship?

"All right, kid, why don't you read some more about
immortal animals," I say,
and pull my knit hat down over my eyes,
blocking out the morning light, blocking out Edward,
blocking out the feeling of something like loss.

# Row

I am lying on Ariana's bed
staring at a ceiling
holding the remnants
of a glow-in-the-dark galaxy.

Kennedy's head is lost in the closet.
"I think I found something."

She wrangles out
a wooden cigar box.

"What is this?"
Kennedy says,
and hands me the box.

It's a box Ariana bought at a thrift store
because she said
it smelled like a lifetime
of memories.

Sweet and acrid.
Pungent and complex.

But I couldn't place the smell
with any single memory.

It wasn't the smell
of the cigar Dad once smoked
that time our uncle returned
from vacation in Cuba.

It wasn't the smell
of our dead mother's perfume,
which she would dab on her wrist
before leaving us alone
with a faceless babysitter.

But maybe it was the smell
of doing something exciting,
of feeling special and wanted.

Maybe it was the smell
of being lived in.

The smell of an object
that harbored secrets
and memories
and weightless things,
like the sound of two girls snuggling.

# Ariana

I wake to the sound of a truck shifting gears, barreling down
the highway in front of us. Edward isn't next to me. But Alex is,
reading a thick British novel. Smelling like dark-roast coffee.

Reminding me of all the times last summer when
the water around us rose up as fog. When sounds of dishes
clattering drifted across the lake from summer cottages
where children lay tucked into bunk beds and life
was absorbed into the shadows of tall trees.

Alex thrums her fingers against the cover of the book,
reminding me of the way she used to thrum her fingers
against a plexiglass hull and the hollow beat
thumped against my core.

Reminding me of the times she'd say one tiny thing,
like, *I'm really glad I came back here this summer,*

and I'd feel our friendship hover momentarily
over our shared sense of loss, like my mother,
like her brother were right there with us.

Last summer, I thought that's what I wanted.
To have a friend who understood. Who experienced
the same feelings as me.

But I feel that sense of hovering again, on this bus, and I try to push it away. It's not what I want now.

Alex turns the page in her book.
She glances over. "Oh, good. You're up."

# Row

I open the lid,
but it's empty.

"I don't get it,"
Kennedy says.
"Why does your sister
keep an empty cigar box
in the depths of her closet?"

"I don't know," I say.

But part of me wonders
if it's because
we all keep
boxes of emptiness
in the depths
of our closets.

I thought that maybe
opening the box
that Ariana keeps
tucked away in the back of her closet
would release all the emotions
we've tucked away

in the back of our minds
since Mom died.

But I open and shut the lid
and I still feel
nothing

because when Mom died,
we cremated our emotions
and scattered them in the ocean
along with the ashes
of her tiny frame.

"It's just a box,"
I say, and hand it back.

# Ariana

"Listen, I hope you don't mind. I asked the kid
to swap seats for a minute, and he got real excited about telling
my roommate about how the Egyptians built the pyramids
pre-invention of the wheel. Apparently they used a lot of boats.

"She's a classics major with a minor in archaeology.
Egyptology is kinda her jam," Alex continues.

*What's college like?* I want to ask her.
*What's your major? How did you decide?*
*Do you think there is a major for people like me,*
*girls with dead mothers?*

But I don't ask Alex any of these questions.
"Yeah, of course," I say. "I feel like
I haven't spoken to you in forever."

"You haven't," Alex says.

I give her a little laugh. But she doesn't think it's funny.

This wasn't supposed to happen in my idea of escaping.
This is not the way this bus ride is supposed to unfold.

I was supposed to watch the snow fall
and the countryside disappear.
Sit idly as nothing happened. Talk to no one.

But Alex sitting next to me is like the moment before
you receive a test back, one you didn't study for,
hoping there's a chance that everything will
work out fine, but knowing that it probably won't.

"Did you know that there are some types of jellyfish
that are immortal?" I say instead.

"Huh?" Alex twists her face at me,
like she's trying to figure out
how jellyfish relate to her unanswered texts.

I point to the animal encyclopedia stuffed
into the seat-back pocket. "It's what they're teaching
kids these days in those things called books."

"Better than teaching them about drugs," Alex says.
Neither of us laughs. But it's funny, in the morbid,
only-funny-to-us kind of way.

"That's messed up," I finally say.
"I know," Alex says.

I forgot how good it feels to feel—
different with someone else.

# Row

Kennedy frowns, but takes the box back.
"How is this not a clue?
It had to contain something, right?"
She flips it around, examining the corners,
still finding nothing.

"What do you want me to do?
Swab it for forensic evidence?
Send it to a lab for DNA testing?

"How is rifling through my sister's closet
going to tell us anything
about where she went?"

Kennedy wedges the box
back into the closet,
then lies down on the carpet,
sighing dramatically.

"You have a good point,
Nancy Drew."

I roll my eyes.
"It's the twenty-first century.
Everyone's secrets are hidden
on their phones."

Kennedy bounces back up.
"Geez, Row. You're a natural,"
Kennedy says, and reaches for her phone.

"Let's scour her socials.
See if she's posted anything
we can use," she says.

# Row

I reach for my phone
and glance at the screen.

I pull up the last text
from Ariana.

Four days ago,
when she was driving home
from the grocery store.

I love you, sis.

Ariana had gone
to the grocery store
to restock
our fridge
with milk and eggs.
She bought us a frozen pizza.
She made me eat a salad.

But Ariana
had come home.

This morning,
there was only one egg left
in the carton
and someone needed
to buy more milk.

Even when we didn't get along,
even when we'd argue over small things
like who ate the last yogurt
or who didn't empty the dishwasher
or who was the reason we were running late
for school,

there was a part of her
that was still my sister.

The part of her
that could text
just to say,

"I love you."

# Ariana

There was nothing magical about that night last summer.
There were no wispy clouds or peppered stars.

I rearranged a row of wooden chairs
in front of a ceremony arch adorned
with wisteria for a wedding
at the Wyndover Lodge while dressed
in an ill-fitting uniform
and faced a losing battle against bugs.

"What are you doing?"
A girl slumped into a seat
in the back row. She unscrewed
a water bottle and drank from it
while following me with her eyes.

She wore beat-up All Stars,
and her hair was all frizzy, like mine.

The bridge of her nose was red and peeling,
and I could see a nasty burn on her shoulders.
I assumed she was a guest of the hotel.
The groom's wayward sister, perhaps.

My coworker returned with two lemonades in hand.
"Oh, hey. Alex meet Ariana.
Ariana, my cousin Alex," she said,
and waved generally in our directions
while ice clinked against the glasses she held.

"Moving these chairs because
guests' thighs might touch," I replied.

"For real?" Alex shaded her eyes with her hand,
like she was trying to inspect the situation.

"Three-inch gaps," my coworker said.
"That's what the bride told us." She set down
the lemonades and rearranged a chair.

"You realize no one's gonna die," Alex said.
I snorted. My coworker stopped what she was doing.
With a short, low hiss, she repeated her cousin's name.

"I'm fine," Alex said.

The way Alex said the word "fine."
The look on her cousin's face in response.

I felt the sense of being misunderstood,
the awkward feeling when other people
desperately want you to be someone different.
Normal. Maybe because you're embarrassing.
Maybe because you're too sad.

"Okay, I'm not fine. Of course I'm not fine.
But it's funny. Right?"

"It's funny," I replied, because I wanted
her to know that I saw her,

not as a tragic story, locked into a genre,
with a formula and an ending.

She almost startled at my response,
like she recognized me, that I wasn't
a stranger she just met for the first time.

"Hey, we're going to a party later.
You should join," she said.

My coworker gave Alex a look
that said, *We're not actually friends.*
*You don't have to invite her.*

But she did, maybe because she needed to know
that there were people in this world
who could understand her.

# Row

"Are these her friends?"
Kennedy says, and I almost forgot
that she was even here.

The screen is a series of photos
of girls I don't know.

I expand a photo to get a better look.

I can tell that these girls
are trying too hard.
The way they tilt their chins
forward and slightly upturned.
The way they smile
and plead for attention.

I glance at my sister's stats.

Ariana has a thousand photos.
Ariana has a thousand followers.
But I'm not convinced that Ariana
has any friends.

Kennedy kinda looks at me
in a way that suggests she knows
something is up.

"Are you all right?"

"Yeah, I'm fine."

"You don't look fine."

She sets down her phone.
"We can talk about whatever is going on.
Because obviously something is going on."

I ignore Kennedy.

It's a serious contradiction,
to want to be heard, to want to be listened to,
to want to feel what I feel without clothing it
in unruffled indifference

and then not letting
Kennedy in.

Why do I act this way?
Why do I say the things
that I say?

Why do words sometimes come to me
all at once like an unstoppable nosebleed,
or sometimes never at all?

Why do we want to be our true, real, full selves,
but only around certain people?

Maybe it's because with sisters,
you can say and be the person you are,
and there's no choice in whether or not
to accept you. They just do,
because you're sisters.

At least that's what
I always believed
would be true.
I thought Ariana and I
had a solid relationship,
that our fights were normal
sisterly fights. About using
all the hot water. About eating
that last yogurt. About who was going
to tell Dad about the nail polish

we spilled on the carpet. Or the soda
we spattered on the wall.

But I don't know what
keeps her up at night.

I don't know whether she worries
about test scores or fitting in
or finding her place
in the world.

It's like Ariana
doesn't want me to know her,
and I don't know if she wants
to know me.

Maybe I shouldn't expect
this much out of my sister.
Maybe I should let
other people in.

Kennedy sits quietly behind me,
watching me scroll
through Ariana's feeds.

She points to more photos
and asks who everyone is.

"I don't know," I say.

I don't know what Ariana sees
for herself next year,

but it scares me,

her leaving.

This time
and forever.

# Ariana

When we arrived at the party, we could hear voices
and music from down the road.

There were acres of land between us
and the next plot, so there was no one
around to tell us to turn the volume down.

The party spilled onto the porch and into the fields.

Inside, I overheard a girl wearing boots
that looked like legitimate work had been done in them
talk about the record labels
and the patriarchal bullshit of the industry.

The room pulsed with confidence.
People had their shit together.
It intimidated me, for sure,
but I also felt this thrilling sense
that maybe this is what life could be like
in five or ten years.

Maybe I would be like the woman
with the loudest laugh in the room,
or the one with stories about
bad dates and terrible bosses.

Maybe instead of trying to make myself small,
I would be the woman
shouldering her way through the crowd,
barking at people as her beer splashed around.

I stood in the kitchen of the farmhouse,
sipping on cheap beer, trying to soak it all in.
Wanting to etch it into my brain
so that I could open it back up
and study this moment like a textbook.

A song came on and it throbbed under my skin,
and I was wedged in a conversation
I only sort of wanted to be in
because it made me feel less of a nobody
in a crowd full of somebodies.

I listened to the song play from the other room,
but no one was dancing.

From across the crowded kitchen, wedged between
the sink and refrigerator, I saw Alex swaying to the beat,
stuck in a conversation she was no longer listening to.

She looked over and saw me watching her,
but instead of feeling embarrassed, I bounced my shoulders
to the beat, and she nodded her head along with me.

Her mouth moved, but I couldn't understand
what she was trying to say,
because all I could hear was the music
seeping into my skin, beating against my chest,
reminding me of what it feels like

to be alive.

## Row

The battery life falls from 10 percent
to 9 while I hold open the phone
and scroll through pages of photos.

I reach one of Ariana's earliest posts.
Six years ago.

A photo of a photo
of Ariana and me
and our mother,

which she printed out
on computer paper
in black and white.

An image missing

the smell of sunscreen,
the sound of our mother laughing,
the taste of salt spray,
the feeling of sand between my toes.

Kennedy leans closer to look at the screen.
"Is that your mom?" she asks.

"Yeah."

"I'm sorry," Kennedy says.

"For what?"

"It's just shitty that you lost your mom."

"There's nothing to apologize about."

"I know. But it sucks."

"It's life," I say.

"It's not fair," Kennedy says.

It wasn't.
It never will be.

Kennedy hands me a cord.
"Here. Use my phone charger."

## Ariana

Alex began showing up to my shift at the Wyndover Lodge
even when her cousin wasn't working.

"So, what do you know about boats?" Alex asked.

"Uh, not much," I said. I didn't want to tell her
that boats reminded me of islands and islands
reminded me of Mom and Mom reminded me of,
well, a lot of things that I didn't want to think about.

"Why?"

Alex hesitated. "Will you come sailing?"

I almost said no, but Alex glanced downward.
I recognized the gesture. When you want something,
so badly, but you're scared of watching for a reaction.
"Sure. I'm off in twenty minutes."

At the public dock, I found Alex tangled in a rope.
"Why the heck do you have a boat?"

Alex mumbled something that sounded like, "I inherited it."

We fumbled with the sails
and floundered our way across the lake,
but eventually we sailed into a cove as daylight clung to the sky
the way a baby clung to its mother,
not wanting to go down for a nap.

"I used to love it here," Alex said,

and I was struck by the way she said the words "used to"
like the way I would occasionally let it slip to strangers,
to people who don't matter that I "used to" live in California,

because packed between those two little words
was a whole history that neither of us was talking about.

# Row

Kennedy is distracted
by the rabbit hole she's entered
scrolling through Ariana's social-media feeds.

My phone is on Ariana's desk,
and my eye lands on an empty spot
on a bulletin board above.

A subtle form of tightness
grows against my chest.

A grainy black-and-white image.
An ultrasound.
A printout that Ariana labeled
*Calamansi*

isn't there.

I run my fingers
over the bare cork.

*Two sisters gone.*

## Row

We were supposed to have
a baby sister.

We were supposed to have
something to love.

But I never got to touch her fuzzy head.
I never saw her feet.

We never had a chance
to call her
sister.

## Ariana

In the cove, there were bugs everywhere,
hungry and eager for blood.

I felt one land on my bare shoulder, exposed,
and open for business like a twenty-four-hour drive-through.

Just as quickly as it landed, it began to stab me
with its needlelike mouthpiece.

I slapped at it and flicked the remnants
of its body into the water below.

"Tiny deaths," Alex said.

"Huh?"

"What you just did."

"Is this some sort of spiritual teaching moment?"

Alex shook her head. "It's just what I've been thinking
for a new song. When is it okay to treat death
as inconsequential? Where do we draw the line
between big deaths and small deaths?
Who gets to define the significance of death?"

I tried to hear the questions turn into lyrics,
to find something resembling a rhythm
in the way she spoke, but that's not what I heard.

It was the hollowness in the words
"death" and "inconsequential"
that I understood, that I could feel,
that I heard so clearly from inside.

"Who did you lose?" I finally asked.

She reached into her backpack and handed me
a can of bug spray. "Oh. I thought you knew."

## Row

I wanted so badly
to experience every aspect
of having a baby sister.

I spent hours imagining her name.

If my baby sister came out with chubby cheeks
and dumplings for legs,
I would name her Calamansi.

If she came out like a little loaf of bread,
I would name her Martha.

If she came out with an elongated torso
and a face that looked like a pickle, she would be Harper.

Dad and Maribel never asked for my opinion.

"We just don't want to be influenced
by anyone else," Maribel would say.
"Like, what if we choose a name
that is the same name as a girl
in your fourth-grade class
who didn't invite you
to her birthday party?"

"Madison? Are you considering
naming her Madison?"

"No, but if we were,
that's exactly the thing
we are worried about."

"Don't name your kid Madison.
She's destined to be a bitch," I said.

"Row. Language," Dad interrupted.

"Okay she's destined to be
not a nice person."

"Well, I can assure you
that Madison is not
on our short list of names."

"What about Amista?" I said.
Amista like our mother.

Neither of them said anything
for a minute.

"Not as a first name,"
Maribel finally responded.
"But maybe a middle name."

"Calamansi Amista Lujan," I said,
and Maribel only gave me a quizzical look.

"You're referring to the fruit?" Dad said.

"Calamansi," Ariana said
as she joined us in the kitchen.

Dad and Maribel looked at each other,
in the kind of way that suggested
they needed to have a talk.

Neither of them was keen on naming
their child after a fruit, but it was trendy
so maybe they should give it some thought?

They never told us her name.

But whatever name
she would have been given,
I knew that to Ariana and me,
she would always be
our Calamansi.

## Ariana

Biology. Genetics. Fate. With all of the discoveries
and vaccines and treatments available in modern medicine,
human beings were not yet smart enough to save everyone.

Was it a matter of studying harder? Or collecting better data?
Or bringing more voices not yet heard into the medical field?

Why are we even here if we are only meant to die?
Is it better to save people from their death,
or prepare us all for the inevitability?

"My brother. Overdose. Five months ago,"
Alex said, staring out onto the water.
"This was his." She waved at the boat and the sails.

"I'm sorry," I said. "That's not enough, I know,
but . . . yeah . . ." I trailed off.

The light in the distance flickered and faded.
The water around us settled into a silent presence,
like fog or heat or smell.

Right after my mother died, I overheard adults
refer to it as "untimely." But what did that even mean?

I loved Mom. I couldn't imagine whether she was 42 or 102
that her death would have hurt any less.

There was no right time for my mother to die,
because when someone we love dies,
it will always be untimely.

I turned back to Alex. My knee grazed against hers.
"I know how it feels," I began to say.
"My mom. Six years ago."

Alex's mouth curled slightly.
"I'm sorry. That sucks, but I could tell
there was something about you that understood."

# Row

I had irrational fears
about Maribel
in the months leading up
to their wedding.

"I'm scared," I said to Dad.
He sat at the dining table
with his laptop, poring over
a contract for a client.

"Mmm" was all I got in response.

"Dad?" I tried again.
He looked up.

"What?" Dad had the look on his face
that he often had ever since we moved here
to Little Lake for his new job.

The face of someone
who was perfectly content
reading legalese
and studying the meaning
of language written
into terms and conditions.

The face of someone
who was actually happy.

I know that what happened to Mom
was an anomaly,
virtually,
statistically
improbable.
But not impossible.

But Dad was bringing someone new
into our lives,
and the same thing
could happen.

Maribel could die.

Dad didn't hear me at all.
"What's up, Row Bow?"

I didn't know where the pain went
that used to lie
on top of Dad's skin.
Like a rash all over his face.
But it hasn't been there for months.

He looked so normal.
He found someone.
He had the chance
to be loved, again.

Maybe strength did come
from burying the past.

Maybe happiness was at the end
of that journey, just like Dad had found.

"Maribel is awesome.
I can't wait
to have her as
a stepmother,"
I said instead,

because looking at my dad now
and knowing how far he had come,
how could I possibly tell him anything
that would jeopardize his face?

Dad closed his laptop
and came over to me on the couch.
He wrapped me in his arms
and smothered me with his
slightly wrinkled shirt.

"You and your sister are the best things
that have ever happened to me."

Sometimes when people hugged me,
it felt too real. Like too much love
contained in one moment.
I didn't want all of my emotions,
sadness and joy,
heartbreak and hopefulness,
to come spilling out of my tear ducts.

Because once they started,
how will they ever
possibly stop?

Even through love, I gritted my teeth.
I took a deep breath,
and I changed the subject.

"Can I buy a new pair of cleats?"

## Ariana

Alex came by the Wyndover Lodge again
to pick up her cousin.

"You want to come to a gig?" Alex said
as I finished folding a crisp white tablecloth.

"A gig?"

"Yeah. We're playing at some party."

"You're in a band?"

"Sort of," Alex said.

Her cousin rolled her eyes.
"They're good. Like record-deal good."

"You have a record deal?" I wanted to ask her
why didn't she tell me. We could talk about her brother,
about my mom, about things
I don't talk about with anyone,
but she couldn't tell me about her record deal?

"They have a song on the radio," her cousin replied,
like she was their manager.
*A song on the radio?* I wanted to scream.

"Then what are you doing hanging around
Little Lake for the summer?" I said, but what I
really meant was, *What are you doing hanging out with me?*

Both Alex and her cousin looked at their feet.
No one responded. They didn't have to.
I understood. It was the same downward glance
that I used to do after my mother died
to avoid talking about things I didn't want to talk about.

Her brother.

We piled into Alex's Jeep and drove to a massive house
in a neighboring town. "A hedge fund manager's son.
He's turning sixteen. Don't judge. They're paying us
good money. Like, more than a decent-size show."

I shrugged. "Good money is good money."
I wasn't judging her choices in gig, but I was judging
our friendship, what I knew. How much I didn't know.

I helped Alex haul in some gear. I took advantage
of the full spread of food and waited with her cousin
until the band made their way to the makeshift stage.
"We're Kickerville Road," one of them said.

The song started up, and I watched the way Alex
no longer looked like the person I knew.
Up there on the stage
Alex was dynamic. Not introspective or quiet.

But as soon as she struck the first chord,
followed by a melodic arrangement,
she wasn't so different.

I looked around at the crowd, trying to see
if anyone noticed, anyone could tell
that the music, it sounded

like the inside of my head.

# Row

Kennedy and I sit cross-legged
on the "Desert Sand" carpet
that Maribel installed
in our bedrooms last summer
replacing the "Smoky Merlot"
that was probably en vogue
when the house was built
in 1980-something.

According to our stepmother,
the new carpeting will show well
"if your father and I ever decide to sell."

Ariana and I exchanged looks
when we learned of the new color scheme,
when we learned that this place
we now call home might someday
no longer be ours.

Kennedy dumps a basket
of paper and recyclables
onto the carpet.

"What are you doing?"

"Ephemera," she says.

"What do you mean?"

"Things that are used or enjoyed
for only a short period of time."

She pulls out a hot-pink sticky note.
"Ephemera," she says again.

"So, basically, you think
that by going through
Ariana's recycling,
we might be able to find some clues?"

"You're on the case, Gumshoe,"
Kennedy replies.

She retrieves a printed assignment.
She finds a grainy black-and-white photo.

"Don't," I say. "Put it back."

Kennedy examines it closely,
even though she knows what it is.

"Is this . . . ?"

"Yes," I say.

"Oh my God.
Is your sister pregnant?"
Her face is a mix of concern
and horror and shock.

"No," I say slowly.
"Maribel is . . . was."

"That's—" Kennedy tries,
but trails off
like everyone,
everyone does.

There are no words.

"I'm sorry."

It hurts in the same way
as all conversations before.
Damp nose. Bulging throat.
Constriction.

"Whatever," I say,
and fall onto the bed,
onto a lumpy pillow

that smells like shampoo,
and swipe to a screen on my phone
and tune out.

# Ariana

"Why do people love this shit?"
Row said, pointing at the radio.

It was Kickerville Road. The song about ghosts.
I wanted it on repeat. I wanted it on surround sound.
I wanted the car next to us to be playing it too.

But Row changed the station,
and then changed it again and again,
until landing on something
that wasn't this song.

Was there a secret language hidden in sounds?
As if the wavelengths could say something
to only some of us.

Because if I closed my eyes
and narrowed in on the chords of the piano,
I was transported somewhere
that wasn't this car,
that wasn't the town of Little Lake.

I was somewhere new,
somewhere significant,
somewhere free.

A car honked behind us
and I stalled out again.
"It isn't shit," I told Row,
and changed the station back.

But she was no longer paying attention to the music.
She was waving her hand at the green light
and the gas pedal and telling me,
"Let's go!"

I turned the key, and the engine sounded like it was crying.
I gave the car too much gas and let off the clutch
too quickly.

We lurched through the stoplight.
Our bodies hurtled forward.

The song ended and the car smoothed
to a steady speed, and we drove straight on the road
that would lead us back to our house.

"I'm glad neither of us became musicians.
The world doesn't need another sad song
about people dying," Row said,
and swung her feet up onto the dash,
socks dropping dried blades of grass.

The sun glared into our eyes. I couldn't look at her.
I didn't understand how she could believe this.
The world *did* need these songs,
because the world needed to know we exist.

## Row

What was it about selling homes
that attracted someone to our family?
Was it because we're a good fixer-upper?

The bones of something that could be
transformed into mid-century modern?
Farmhouse chic? Boho contemporary?

"I think they're serious," Ariana said.

We tried to ignore Dad and Maribel
sautéing garlic in the kitchen.
We tried to ignore the second pour of wine
and the clink of glasses.

I was trying to find the value for "x"
while Ariana was trying to eavesdrop.
"Dad's going to ask her to marry him,"
she whispered.

"Did he say that?" I whispered back.

Dad opened a package of linguine
with too much vigor.
Pasta flew everywhere.

The sound of the dried strands
falling to the floor was what I imagined
a tiny army of ants might sound like
if they fell from the sky
and invaded our kitchen.

"Oh shit," he said,
and Maribel laughed,
and they both crouched to the floor
to pick up the pasta, out of view.
I imagined that they might be kissing.

Ariana shook her head.
"Just look at him.
He's happy."

I shifted the weight of my body
around on the stiff wooden chair.
A small act of change.
Like an accumulation of small changes
that I had somehow missed
all around me.

People in this family
could be happy.

# Ariana

I kept listening to Kickerville Road on repeat.
Their demo album. The EP.
Tracks from their unreleased
studio album that Alex gave me.

I wanted to know what it was like to be a girl like Alex,
someone who feels the same gutting sense of loss that I did
and yet still makes the kind of music that burrows into your brain
like creatures in a lonely forest looking for a home.

There's something I need to do. Will you come with me?
Alex texted. I didn't know what kind of friend I was to Alex,
if I was the only person she turned to
when she needed
to feel the loss of her brother,
like I was her emotional support animal.

But I agreed to meet her for a hike, even though
I knew it had something to do with her brother.

We crossed a stream.

My toe faltered and my shoe fell in.
But I plowed ahead with a soggy sock
and a heart that felt overgrown.

We stopped at a spot where the trail opened up
and an outcrop of rocks basked in full sun.

Alex pulled out a small plastic container from her backpack,
one you might use to store leftovers,
but the insides were gray and blackened.

"My brother," she said.
"Not all of him, but enough."

I remember scattering my mother's ashes.
At the time I thought it was some sort of magic.
Her body becoming one with the earth.

Ashes to ashes, dust to dust, and all that.

I remember the wind took all of the ashes
and blew them around with the sand and the salt-spray air,
and I covered my nose in fear of breathing too much of her in.

I used to believe that was how life and death
were always meant to be.

Commingling like a swirl of dust in the wind,

and every time I saw the wind kick up,
I thought about Mom.

But there was nothing magical about death,
because there is no magic in being human.

Alex tried to get the wind to do the same thing,
but there wasn't even a breeze
and she tried to sprinkle a clump of ash into the air,
but it fell like a clod of dirt back onto the rocky ground.

There on the top of a rock, blazing in the sun,
were the cremated remains of Alex's brother.

We both stared at the thin layer of gray ash on top of gray rocks.

I could have offered her advice on how to scatter ashes;
suggest that we climb higher, find a cliff,
go somewhere other than this clearing, with no breeze,
no room for the wind to catch hold of someone's soul.

I could have suggested we abandon this effort
and instead launch her brother's dinghy
and wait for the wind to carry away the ashes
the way the wind carries away the sails.

But I didn't say anything,
because this moment didn't need

to be carefully crafted with the perfect gust of wind
or timed with the right filter of light.

The sun bore down on us,
vegetation wilted in the heat,
and I stood awkwardly,
continuing to watch Alex falter.

She dumped the remaining contents
onto a patch of dirt near a pine tree.

"This is where we used to play," she muttered.
"Who knew that the brother
you used to climb trees with,
pretend to be pirates and monsters and dragons with,
would turn out to . . ."

Alex didn't finish.

But I knew how the story ended.
I knew that the monster ate him alive,
the pirate drowned him at sea.

That as kids we could be heroes in our own stories.
That we could never be defeated by anything
until our world stopped being imaginary,
and the giant fought back,
and the monsters came out to eat us.

# Row

"How far along was she?"
Kennedy fingers the image,
tracing the outline of a nose.

"Fifteen weeks," I say.

Kennedy looks up.
"Wait, fifteen weeks?
That's a really long time."

Kennedy doesn't go anywhere,
but it's like her body is cycling
around the room.
"You didn't tell me for
four whole months
that your stepmother
was pregnant?

"Were you ever going to tell me?

"Was I supposed to just show up here
one day and hear a baby crying
and, like, ask you how it got here?

"I can't believe I didn't even notice.
I'm going through all the times
I saw Maribel and didn't say anything."

Kennedy waves the sonogram at me.
"Seriously, Row. What the hell?"

# Ariana

"Why are you hanging out with her again?" Row said
while lying on the couch, tossing a soccer ball in the air.

"I thought you didn't even like her," Row continued.

"I never said that. What gave you that impression?"

"Uh. You actually did say that. Last week.
I said you should invite your new friend
to hang out over here, and you said,
'We're not really friends.'"

"I said that?" I was surprised I admitted it
out loud to Row. The question had been there,
but it wasn't something I wanted anyone to know.
That the more we hung out,
the less of a friend I felt like to Alex.

Row balances the ball on her feet,
outstretched in the air
as she lies on her back.

She's trying to make it spin
without crashing on top of the coffee table.

I try to change the subject.
"Maribel doesn't want you doing that."

"Why do you spend so much time with her
if you're not friends with her?

"Is it because she's in a mildly famous band?"

"No," I scoffed.

"Is it because her brother died?"

"Jesus, no."

"I wouldn't blame you if that were the reason,"
Row says quietly.
"No one understands us."

# Row

Kennedy's face is tight with concern.
But I can't. Look at her.
The image of our sister.
The only photo we will ever have.
She's . . . What is the verb for "death via miscarriage"?

"Row."

I slide open my phone.
"I'm busy."

Kennedy glances at my screen.
"Row! What are you doing?"

"What do you mean?"

"We need to talk."
She points to my screen live streaming
the English Premier League.
"This isn't talking."

"It's Liverpool versus Manchester City."

"Yeah, I can see."

"But Salah has the ball."
The Liverpool forward
is in front of the goal.
He takes two touches
to get around the City defenders.
He drives one in
but can't keep it under
the crossbar.

The ball sails behind the goal.

"Row, I need us to talk."

And I need Ariana
to waltz into her room,
flop onto the bed,
and pull out her phone
like nothing ever happened.

I absolutely need
to sit here on the carpet
and watch Liverpool crush Manchester City
and not be worried about anything.

# Ariana

"Where are you going?" Maribel asked again.
I rummaged through a pile of shoes by the front door,
trying to find a pair that would best go unnoticed.

I didn't want my shoes or anything
to say too much about me.

"It's just one county over. They're playing a show.
I'll be home by midnight."

Maribel looked over at Dad, who was concentrating
hard on the player at bat on the screen.

"Dad said I could go."

Maribel continued to look at Dad.
"He did, did he?"
Dad said nothing.

"Can I go?" Row perked up,
her head peeking over the back of the couch.

"No," Maribel, Dad, and I all responded.

"Why not?"

"For starters, you've got a tournament
tomorrow morning." Dad finally pulled his eyes
away from the screen and patted Row on the shoulder.

"Oh, right." Row slouched further
into the couch cushions.

I went back to my room to find a pile of crap
I had thrown on my bed as provisions. Sunscreen.
Sunglasses. Cash. Lip balm. A phone charger.
A lighter I wasn't intending to use because I had never
actually smoked anything, tucked into the
pocket of my purse, just in case,
you know, someone asked for a light.

Row followed me and plopped herself on top of
the pile of stuff. I tried to roll her body away.

"Should I quit soccer?"

"Why?" I stuffed the contents on the bed
into a small leather purse I found at Goodwill.

"Because I might be missing out
on quintessential moments of teenage life."

"But don't you love playing soccer?"

"Yeah, but what if I love other things too?

"Like you have all this time to explore
other things in life. To find out stuff
that you might love that you otherwise
would never have known."

I didn't know how to respond to Row,
because I wasn't off finding out if I loved
soccer or swimming,
or pottery or poetry.

What my little sister didn't realize
was that while she was off playing soccer,
I was doing nothing.

I had no hobbies.
No sports.
No extracurricular interests.

What was I doing?
I didn't even know.
Maybe scrolling through socials
wondering what it was like to be living
some kind of best life?

Maybe wondering what it would be like
to be a girl with a mother.

Maybe wondering if I was someone
who could even sustain a friendship
with someone like Alex.

If I were actually her friend, there for the good times
and the bad, instead of just the bad.

"You're just so good at soccer,"
I eventually said.

Row rolled her eyes and sat up on the bed.
"Yeah, that's not helpful.
Of course I'm good at soccer.
I've practiced every day for, like, nine years.
Anyone who devotes that much time to something
is going to be good.
I just wanted you to, like, give me
some wise sisterly advice, or something."

I tried to act like I *did* just give her
some wise sisterly advice.
That her words didn't get to me.
I tried to smile and shrug and quickly grab
the purse and the car keys and tell her

I had to run.

But I couldn't shake the question
from my head. How could Row continue
to wake up and go to practice every single day,
how could Alex continue to get up on a stage
that she once shared with her brother,

when I had spent, not days or months,
but years doing nothing?

*How could I be so different?*

# Row

"How are you unfazed by all of this?
Your sister is gone.
Your house is in disarray,
and you just told me that your
stepmother has been pregnant
for months. Until now.

"This is bad, Row."
She waves at the room,
at ourselves.

"Sometimes," Kennedy huffs,
"I hear the girls on the soccer team
talk about you.
Like you're this superhero
because when you take a nasty tumble
on the turf, one bad enough
to solicit audible gasps
from the crowd,
you get up without so much
as a grimace."

She shakes her head
and rolls her eyes.
"But I know
your badass-soccer-phenom persona
is just a front.
That there's stuff
that truly
rattles you."

She points to the image
of my former sister.

"You're still the same person
who cried the first time
you spent the night at my house.
My mom had to drive
back to your house
in her pajamas
and pick up Ariana
because you wouldn't sleep
at my house
without her."

"I told you never
to tell anyone about that," I say.

"I'm not.
I'm telling you.
Reminding you.

"I know that you have
this special bond
with your sister.
That she's your emotional confidante.
But maybe it's not healthy
to live with such extremes."

I don't respond.
I just sit on the carpet
picking at tufts.

Kennedy stands up.
"There are other people
you can share stuff with."

I look up at her, standing by the door.
"Where are you going?"

Kennedy mutters,
"I've gotta pee."

# Row

On the screen of my phone,
City takes a shot on goal,
but it's straight into the hands
of the Liverpool keeper.

The players on both teams
jog closer to the midfield,
as the goalie sets up a kick.

Kennedy returns
from the bathroom
and looks at my phone.
"Soccer. It's always
soccer with you."

She sits down
on the carpet
right in front of me,
pulls out her phone,
and turns the screen around
so it's right next to mine.

So I can't avoid
seeing her screen.

Kennedy:    Can I borrow your copy of the
                    physics study guide?
Ariana:      Sure. It's on the desk in my
                    room.

"Tell me. Why is your sister
responding to me if
she's supposed to be missing."

"She's not missing.
I told you she's gone."

Kennedy lowers her phone,
and I lower mine.
She speaks slowly,
like she's trying to stay calm,
but her jaw is clenched,
facial muscles tight.

"Why haven't you just called her?"

I don't say anything.

"What the hell
have we been doing?"
Kennedy bursts.

"It was your idea.
This whole Nancy Drew thing."
My voice is five octaves higher.

"Yeah, because I didn't know
that 'gone' meant
you're just not talking to her.
I thought 'gone' meant
maybe something bad."
Kennedy took a breath.

I still don't say anything.
Picking at the carpet.
Leaving my mark on the floor.

Kennedy studies me,
but I don't know
what she can learn.

"You think that no one
other than Ariana
can ever understand
the depth of your emotional pain.
But I see you. A lot of us
have been there.
Different circumstances,
same pain."

Kennedy stands up.
She steps over a pile of socks
waiting to be laundered
and hangs at the edge of the door.

"Pain doesn't always
make someone a sympathetic character.
Sometimes pain just turns you
into a bitch."

## *Ariana*

A late-summer storm rolled through that evening
and the rain left a layer of gloss on the road.

Eight of us piled into Alex's Jeep,
heading to a show at a venue in a nearby town.

But she took a curve down the wooded back road
with too much speed, and I felt the car glide on two wheels
while those of us crammed in the back seat, in the trunk,
and unrestrained inside the Jeep
hovered momentarily above the leather interior,
holding our breaths.

No one screamed like we should have.

No one said a word as we drove on two wheels.
Life scraped the asphalt in that moment,
and when the Jeep landed with an uncomfortable *thud*,
we landed upright on the road in our lane, and alive.

When we pulled up to the venue, everyone scrambled out.
"Shit, we're so late," I heard someone say.

Alex threw me the keys and ran for the stage door.
"Can you unload the merch?"

The white lines on the asphalt had faded.
The corners of the cardboard box holding T-shirts had collapsed.
I stared into the trunk of the Jeep and caught my breath,

trying to focus on the steady beat of my heart.

## Row

I hear the sound of Kennedy's socks
shuffling down the hall.
I hear the sound of her pulling on boots,
the sound of a door opening,
but I can't hear the sound
of the snow falling
and piling outside.

Kennedy leaves

and I watch Salah drive one in
on the screen. A shot that sails
into the upper-right corner
that no keeper could touch.
I see the Liverpool fans rise
and wave their scarves
as the weather in England
turns from
sleet into snow.

I don't know why any of this
happened,
but it did.

I don't know why
anyone dies.

But they do.

## Ariana

I always imagined that having a great friend
would be like re-watching your favorite movie.
Where you could finish each other's lines.
Know exactly what was going to happen
and still get to cry and laugh at all your favorite parts.

But it wasn't like that with Alex.
The more I hung out with her, the less I understood her.
It was like I could spend an infinite amount of hours
and still wouldn't get what she was about to say
or know when our favorite parts would even happen.

She was ecstatic when I was annoyed.
She was oblivious when I was hurting inside.

She never seemed to have this looming sense of dread
about the next moment the way I did,
and the way life seemed to burst at the seams all around her,
I wanted to sew it all back up and hide.

As I watched Alex up there on the stage,
the way her body stood poised,
with a guitar in hand, the way she looked
so present with the audience and the music,

the way joy landed on her face
with every holler, every cheer,
every stomp of feet from the crowd,

even as she stood next to an empty space
once occupied by her brother,

it wasn't an act.
This was her.

I found myself wondering why so much life
could exist within one person,
how her pain wasn't hidden or buried—
it was transformed.

The song ended, the crowd grew quiet, the lights
changed from yellow to blue,
and Alex stepped up to the mic.
"This one's about ghosts."

The drummer counted off the song.
I saw Alex glance ever so slightly
over to the empty space next to her,
like she was saying something directly to him.

Then she took her arm and she ripped it.
The chord reverberating against the floor, the ceiling,
and all the walls in the venue.

The crowd cheered, and into the mic
Alex belted out the opening lines to the song,
low and guttural, and maybe,
a music critic might write, haunting.

But it wasn't like that for me.

Listening to the music,
feeling the sway of bodies around me,
I wasn't transported to an otherworldly place,
where we could connect deeper, more meaningfully
with those we love and have loved.

I was eleven years old and I was stuck in the moment
where all I could hear was the sound of the frother steaming milk,
a barista's harried voice speaking to an operator
on the other end of her cell phone,
and my mom.

My mom.

# Row

I once told a therapist
that when I'm sad, I play soccer,
and she thought that was
an excellent coping strategy.
She told me about all the benefits
of exercise and endorphins
on feelings of depression,
anxiety, and stress.

Maybe if she were here now,
that same therapist
would see me pulling
on my joggers,
searching for my cleats,
throwing a ball into a bag,
and think:

*This young woman is productively
applying a coping strategy to manage
her feelings of sadness.*

Because that's what
it can look like
to everyone else.

Except Kennedy.
Except Ariana.
Except me.

# Ariana

Even Elisabeth Kübler-Ross doesn't believe
in the five stages of grief, and she wrote them.

I have felt all the emotions in the Kübler-Ross model.
From bargaining to acceptance, depression to anger.

Sometimes even denial.

But Kübler-Ross admits there is no set path
to move through grief. No linear structure.
There isn't even a contained set of emotions.

What about sardonic? What about skeptical?
What about anxiety, fear, and loneliness?
What about love?

We don't talk enough about love. Love in relation to grief.
It hurts to think about the people we love.

It hurts so much to know that the hearts of people we loved,
once soft and pliable, are now buried in the cold, hard ground.

# Row

I don't know why
someone gets out of bed
in the middle of a snowstorm
and walks outside.

At least, I say I don't
understand, but I do.

It's the same reason
I'm out here
in joggers
and cleats
with new snow
falling onto
soft pillowy mounds,
and me
dribbling
fruitlessly
up and down the field.

Because something
inside us
compels us to be here,
to be there,
to be wherever
we need to be

where we don't have to be fine.

I'm not fine.
No one was fine.

I rip a shot.
It's six inches wide.

I look around and no one is here.
"Mom, you're supposed to be helping."

# Ariana

"What did you think?" Alex twisted the cap
on a plastic water bottle. Beads
of condensation formed on the sides.

I couldn't tell her that I felt like a box of loose
puzzle pieces. That I didn't feel like I was here,
in this cramped space, behind the stage,
where guys were moving around
instruments and equipment and coiling up cables.

Someone offered us beer.
Alex shook her head. "Driving,"
she said, pointing to the water.
I took the can and cracked it open,
but left it untouched by my side.

I wondered if Alex sang to herself alone
in front of a mirror, trying to get the song right,
finding a way to sing in order to take us somewhere.

I wondered if Alex rehearsed the song about ghosts
the way that doctors rehearsed the words
they must say to a child whose mother has died.

Every hospital has a room reserved
for conversations about death.

A space with four chairs, one for each of us
but no place for Mom.

When they were playing that song
the keyboardist was pounding,
the drummer was beating,
Alex was wailing,
but I couldn't hear any of them.

All I could hear, echoing off the walls,
were the words repeated,

"I'm sorry. I have bad news. Your mother died today."

"What did you think?" Alex said again.
Her face was contorted. The high of being up there
onstage starting to fade.

"Do you practice singing that way?"

"What do you mean?"

"You know, with all that grief?"

"Do I practice singing with grief?"

She rolled her eyes and didn't say anything,
and maybe if I had just left it at that,
we would have never stopped talking.

"Because it looks rehearsed."

"Seriously? You of all people are telling me
that my grief looks rehearsed."

I felt the ends of my nerves run hot.
Alex's brow furrowed.

Some people got stress lines on their foreheads
if they worked too hard, but Mom called them trophy lines.
Each one earned through kicking ass.

I'm stuck remembering my mom's face.
The brow lines left permanently furrowed.
All of her trophies etched across her face
when she died.

I missed her so much. I didn't know
what to do with the pain.

I thought I liked having a friend who understood,
but I didn't. Alex understood in a way
that I wanted to forget.

I never felt like I had the space to move forward
with Alex, to grow beyond my grief.

I felt like that's what she was doing with me.
Using me to help her heal but not allowing me
to do the same. I didn't like this anymore.

"It just seems a little inauthentic," I said.

"Ariana, stop being a bitch.
You're better than this." Alex stood up
and wandered over to some of her other friends.

I should have been better than this.
I should have normal reactions to watching a friend
sing a song up onstage. But I wasn't normal,
and I wasn't sure I was even a friend.

# Row

Before Mom died,
she had to work late,
or needed to call a client,
or was out of town on business travel.

She never made it to a game.

But after she died, she came back.
*That* kind of back.
The supernatural kind.
Back to play soccer.

When the balls of my feet
run up and down
the cut-grass field,
she is there
running through me.

So clearly, so viscerally
through every pass
and every play.

And I never want
to stop playing,
stop being there
with Mom,

because when the game is over
and I leave the field,
Mom doesn't follow.
She never drives home.
She never hugs Dad or Ariana.

She just stays trapped on the pitch,
waiting for me to return.

I never want to stop playing,
because every time I do,
it feels like
she dies
all over
again.

# Ariana

"You are the last person I expected to see.
Probably ever," Alex begins. "You said
some pretty shitty things to me. It wasn't cool."

Looking at Alex is like staring into a pool
of gray water of unknown depth.

"I get it," Alex continued. "I know where
you're coming from. The impulse to direct pain
on someone else. We could have talked about it.

"But a whole month went by
and you never once returned
any of my texts or phone calls
or even the letter I snail mailed,
not out of desperation but out of hope
that the invisible threads that held us
together would still be there."

Alex shakes her head. She fumbles
with the pages of her book.
"You never fricken responded.

"I guess I expected you to be a better friend,"
she says low and soft, the way she sometimes sings
the band's most poignant lyrics.

*That's what I expected from you, too*, I don't say.

I know why I stopped returning her texts, because
when I was around her I felt so one-dimensional.

*I am the girl with the dead mother.*

I thought I wanted a friend like Alex, not only because
she understood loss, but also because she understood
the feeling of being defined by one thing.

But that's not who she is. When Alex was up on the stage,
she refused to be defined solely by her grief,

but I felt like I wasn't allowed to be defined
by anything other than mine.

Outside the window, the traffic is increasing.
Buildings appear. Strip malls guide our way into the city.

"I feel like you were only friends with me
because my mom died," I finally admit.

Alex immediately starts talking again.
"That's not true. How could you even say that?"

The bus slows as the cars thicken.

"Ariana, you need to let go. It helps. It really does.
I miss my brother every day,
but with music, the band, and college—
life didn't stop without my brother."

## Row

No one.
Not Dad.
Not Kennedy.
Not Ariana.
Knows about Mom.

Because Mom returned
to be with me.
But why?

Because I believe in ghosts?
Because I believed all those stories
Mom would tell us
about the dead people
who came to visit her?

"They live with us everywhere,"
she used to say to me, long before she died.

I thought she meant "us"
as in the universal.
Us as in *everyone*.

But maybe she only meant
"You and me."

Not Dad.
Not Ariana.

Not anyone else in this family.

Just us.

# Ariana

I pause two seconds too long, and my window
of response disappears. The words I want to tell Alex
slip back into my throat, down into my stomach,
churning and stewing alone.

Edward hovers behind Alex, clutching
a thick illustrated volume about pyramids.

"I want to eat my fruit snacks," Edward announces.
Alex stands up, and it's like all those invisible threads
that once connected us finally stretch too far,

                                finally snap,

because before she leaves, Alex says,

"Your mom died, but your life didn't stop.
You're just too scared to let yourself figure it out."

# Row

I shag the wayward ball
and tee it up for another shot.

It's Mom who I can count on,
always on the field,
to be there for me.

I dribble the ball from midfield,
closing in on the goal.

"We'll get it this time,"
I tell her.

I wind up a shot,
and when the ball hits
the sweet spot on my laces,
I know it's going to sail in.

Upper left.
Missing the goalpost.
It hits the back of the net.

I go in for another one
and another, and there we are on the field
zigzagging lines in the snow,
smacking sick shots into the goal.

It feels so good.

Until I pause from inside the goal,
retrieving the ball,
and look out onto the white expanse.

The field is empty.
The parking lot is covered in snow.
There are trails of my footprints,
and my bag sits on a solitary bench.

No one else is here.

"Mom?"

No one answers.

"Mom, where's Ariana?"

No one answers.

I wish that Mom could talk to me.
I wish that she could tell me what to do
about Ariana, about Dad, about Kennedy,
about pain.

But she can't talk
because she's dead,
and Ghost Mom never says anything.

She only plays soccer.

"Mom, I need you."

No one answers.

# Row

"Are you even here?" I shout.

No one can hear me.

"Why can't you answer me?"
*She's dead, you idiot.*

*Why can't you be here for me,
for us, for Ariana?*

For six years I've been asking that question,
but no one will give me an answer.

*Why did you have to die?*

I run the ball back out of the penalty box.
My foot plants itself on the ground.
It hits something underneath the snow.

My ankle turns.
Body off-balance.
I collapse into the snow.

It's like all those times
you fall in a game
and the ref halts the play
and your teammates gather around you
and the trainer runs onto the field
with the first-aid kit

asking you,

"Where does it hurt?"

"Everywhere,"
you mumble.

"I didn't catch that.
Can you say it again?"
the trainer says.

"Ankle," you repeat.
"Just give me a minute."

And you lie there waiting
for the throbbing to subside,
but it never does.

Eventually you pull yourself up
and hobble off the field.

You want your mom to be there
to help you, but she can't.

Because even Ghost Mom
can't stop the pain.

# Ariana

I can live a better life if I just tried harder?
Is that what Alex is trying to tell me? Get over it.
Move on. Be more like her? Even with Alex
I feel like my grief makes her uncomfortable.

Why couldn't she just let me be the person who I am?
Why can't I just feel the feelings that I have?

I try to shift around in my seat, but the painting
leaves me no room, and I feel confined like a sleeping bag,
shoved into a stuff sack.

Edward reaches under his seat for his backpack.
The slow whine of every zipper opening and closing,
sounds like a cacophony of desperate people crying.

The crinkle of plastic. The chewing. The smell
of bodies perspiring all around me.

I don't know anything about Edward.
Whether he has a good family, a good home.
I don't know why he or any of us is here on this bus.

What desperate situation drew us to leave in a snowstorm?
To put our lives in the hands of a driver?
To be protected only by a sign posted up front
that reads, YOUR SAFETY IS OUR NUMBER ONE CONCERN.


Because is it?


Edward stuffs a whole handful of fruit snacks
into his mouth. "Do you want to know
the one thing in this world I can't live without?"

Edward is bouncing in his seat.
"Not really," I say.

"It's my sister," he says, and continues.
Chewing. Bouncing. Talking.

Edward turns to me. "What's the one thing in the world
you can't live without?"

I sigh. I look out the window. "Breathing," I say.
Edward inhales and exhales and scrunches up his face.

"Why?"

"Because we literally can't live without breathing."

The weight of the painting grows on my legs.
I lift it and try to put it on the floor. But then
my legs have nowhere to stretch, so I just hold
it in the palms of my hands. Hovering above my knees.

Edward stops chewing. "But why?"

"Why do we breathe? I don't know.
So that we can live."

"But why?" Edward is bouncing again.

"Because if we don't live, we die," I say.

Edward stops bouncing.

"Everyone?" I hear him say, but I'm distracted
by the scene outside. The long shadows from tall buildings.
Garbage trucks and taxicabs. Stoplights and storefronts
and humans walking around with their phones.

"Yeah, everyone dies," I say, without thinking.

"Even my sister," Edward says so quietly
that maybe he didn't intend for me to hear.

But I heard him. I heard the pain, the grieving.
I heard him say something with his kid heart
that I once felt in mine.

It aches so deep. The pain so real. Rising upward. Rising higher.
Until it surfaces. Finally given a chance to breathe.

                                             "Yep. She'll die too."

The words escape. I can't haul them back.
I can't swallow hard enough to unsay them.

The pain comes out so flippant.
So callous. Biting. With lots of sharp teeth.

I look over at Edward.

He's frozen. There's a wad of fruit snack stuck in his cheek.
He's staring blankly at the seat in front of us.
Eyes so wide. Too wide.

"I didn't . . ." But I stop. I don't have any idea what to say
to fix this. I watch his tiny body crumple.

I watch what the words I said do to his face.
His muscles are too weak. Too unprepared to hold it all in.
He starts crying, and it breaks me.

The bus is rumbling through the city in spurts and jolts,
but Edward jumps out of his seat and is running up the aisle,
swaying back and forth with the twists
and turns of the city streets.

Everyone is looking at him. Everyone is looking at me.

His mother is yelling at him to stop.
The bus driver is yelling at him to stay in his seat.

But he continues to scream and cry.
Finally, Alex reaches her arms into the aisle
and catches Edward as he tries to run past.

Alex picks up Edward as he's kicking and screaming
and delivers him back into the lap of his mother.

# Row

I've had more ankle sprains
than is reasonable for someone my age.

*Overuse.*
*Understretching.*
*Weak ankles.*
*Not enough icing.*

If only we could tend to our grief
the way we tend to our injuries:
the physical therapy,
the ice packs.

If only there were doctors
who were trained in this type of healing,
the ones who could tell you
that you'd be back on the field
in two weeks, as long as you follow
their regimen.

But there is no healing process
when irreversible things happen,
like mothers dying.

No way to heal
things that can never be undone.

# Ariana

As soon as we arrive in the city, I gather my things,
the painting stuffed under my arm,
and try to get off that bus as fast as I can.

But Edward's mother stops me. "What is wrong with you?"
What kind of person makes an eight-year-old cry?"

I look at the floor. Caked in dirt that came from our shoes.
Rings of salt from the roads. "I'm sorry."

"She's sick," Edward's mother says, pointing at the baby,
"and you just told my son that his sister is going to die?"

"I didn't know," I say. Edward's face peeks out
from behind his mother. He doesn't know the question
to ask, but I can see in his eyes that he's saying,
*Why did you hurt me?*

"I'm really sorry, Edward," I tell him. He doesn't react.
Just keeps staring at me with longing eyes. Wanting to know
when it will all stop hurting.

I try again. "I hurt you. That's not right. I'm sorry."
Edward gives me an almost imperceptible nod.

It's still not okay. His life might not be okay.
His sister might die. Tomorrow or in eighty years,
and it will still never be okay.

Edward's mother grabs hold of his hand and hauls
her children away. They disappear into the bus station.
Into the flurry of people and hustle
moving in every direction.

# Row

It's frankly pretty challenging
to hobble through the snow
with a sprained ankle,
so by the time I end up on the doorstep,
I feel hot, throbbing pain inside my snow boot.

Kennedy answers with her little brother, Lincoln,
wrapped around her like a full-grown sloth.

"Hey," she says. She's trying to be nice
in front of Lincoln. But her expression
is tired. Annoyed. Unsurprised.

"I think I sprained my ankle."

"Again?"

"It hurts," I say.

Kennedy cocks her head,
like she's searching my face
for the words she wants me to say.

But I don't know how to tell her.

Lincoln slides off,
scrambling away
into the depths
of the house.

"My mom isn't here,"
Kennedy says.
"She had to take an extra shift
at the hospital because of the weather."

I swallow, but my throat is dry.
"That's okay."

Kennedy doesn't move.
Hand still holding the door.
"Why didn't you tell me, Row?"

I didn't want to tell anyone.
It felt too precious, too fragile.
The sense of hope. The possibility of love.

My words come out so cautious.
Like footsteps on the ice.

"Maybe if we didn't love her as much.
Maybe if we didn't stake all of our
hopes and dreams on her,
she would have lived.

"But she died, Kennedy."

# Ariana

Outside the bus, Alex is waiting. "Seriously, Ariana.
He was such a sweet kid. Maybe a little annoying. But really?"

I want to let go. I want to explore life and be a better person.
I want to chase after life like my little sister out on the field.
I want to be whoever it is I am supposed to be.

Of course I do.

But I can't be this. Who I just was five minutes ago.
A person who could cause such pain to a kid like Edward.
I nod back at her. "I know. It's not okay."

We are so different. In our pain. In our grief.
But Alex doesn't see my pain. The hurt, not from grief,
but from us. A friendship I wanted—I needed—
that never happened.

She doesn't recognize the way pain, which we both possess,
wants to mirror itself on someone else. On me. On strangers.

Maybe Alex could only see me as the girl with the dead mother
because that's all I could see of myself. But I wanted
to at least try to be someone more. Someone with multitudes.

"I thought that our friendship would help me move on.
But sometimes, the way you dismissed the way I felt,
even today, it hurt," I say.

Alex looks like she wants to say something,
but her roommate wanders back to us.
"We need to go," her roommate says.

"I'm so much more than the girl who lost her mother,"
I say. "I wish you could have seen that."

Alex looks like the girl that I sometimes saw.
The girl whose hand trembled as she tried
to scatter her brother's ashes. The girl who wanted,
even on the hottest days, to wrap herself
in a ratty old sweatshirt because maybe
it still held on to the scent of her brother.

But she was also the girl up onstage,
who could command a crowd, close her eyes,
and take us all somewhere with her songs.

She shifted the guitar case strapped to her back.
"I'm sorry, Ariana. Maybe it is true. I only saw you
as my friend who understood the experience of loss."

Her roommate looks at her watch
and whispers again, "We really have to go."
Alex nods.

Even though our relationship never became
the kind of friendship with layers like sedimentary rock,
I still appreciated what Alex brought to my life,
the complexity of who she could be,
the idea that I didn't have to be one thing either.

Before she heads for the subway, I call out,
"Play the one about ghosts tonight, okay?"

Alex looks confused at first. Then her face softens.
"We always do."

# Row

"I'm sorry I didn't tell you,"
I say quietly.

"It was a girl?"

I nod.

"It must hurt."

I nod.

Kennedy opens the door
wider. Warm air
touches my face.

Inside I see
there are plates
and dirty dishes.

Piles of mail.
Snow boots
and streaks of mud.

Plastic trucks
and picture books
scattered about the floor.

"I can probably figure out
how to wrap your ankle
by googling it or something,"
Kennedy says.

I hobble inside.

Kennedy disappears
into the kitchen and returns
a few minutes later
with an elastic bandage wrap
tucked under her arm
and two mugs of cocoa.

We both blow on our mugs,
cooling the surface.

It tastes like campfires,
and cabins,
and friendship bracelets.

It tastes like French braids
and flashlights
and sleepovers.

Kennedy is still quiet.

"Do you believe
in ghosts?" I say finally.

She hesitates for a moment.
Really considering the question.

"I think so? My mom does
for sure. She says her mother
comes to visit her." Kennedy pauses,
then continues. "At the most
inopportune moments. Like when
she's sitting on the toilet
and stuff like that."

I snort and almost spill
the cocoa. "Weird."

"Yep," Kennedy says.

She hesitates.
"Why? Do you?"

I set the mug down
on the coffee table
and fiddle with the wrap,
tightening and retightening
the bandage. Then,
after a while,
I nod.

"She's there with me
when I play."

"Your mom?" Kennedy.

I nod. "My soccer-playing
ghost mom."

Kennedy takes another sip of cocoa,
and I don't need her
to do anything more
than be here
and listen.

## Row

After we finish our hot chocolate,
Kennedy hesitates. "I found her."

"Ariana?"

Kennedy nods.

"How?"

She hands me
a piece of paper.

I recognize the format.
It's a transcript
printed on our school's
distinctive
watermarked blue paper.

"It was underneath
the sonogram,"
Kennedy says.

My sister's grades
look like a Scrabble hand.
Too many consonants.
Not enough vowels.

I read a handwritten note.

*Ariana, please consider my offer to show*
*your work at the gallery exhibition on Saturday.*

"I did some legit sleuthing."
Kennedy smiles.
"You should have seen me.
It was pretty dope.
Called up some contacts.
Followed some leads."

I hand the transcript back.

"She went to the city," Kennedy says.

# Ariana

"There's a spot on the wall over there," a girl with red and pink and orange hair says. "A few people couldn't make it.
Because of the snow."
She hands me a sheet of instructions.
"This your first show?"

I nod. It's my first time feeling so exposed, I want to tell her.

"Mine too," she says, then sort of falters. "I'm a little nervous about my parents seeing my work."

She points to a sculpture that is loud and angry and beautiful.
Broken green and brown bottles.
Shards of glass. Arranged in a way
like an overflowing garden fountain.
All jutting out, wanting to stab you.
"They're making me put caution tape around it," she says.

"Probably best no one dies tonight," I reply.
The girl with multicolored hair grins so wide. "Touché."

# Row

"There's still time to make it down there."
Kennedy glances at her watch.
"I looked at the bus schedule.
One leaves in half an hour."

"I said hurtful things to Ariana," I say.
"I implied that something is wrong
with her. Like as a person. Like her feelings
were something other than human emotion."

Kennedy stops and contemplates for a minute.

"Maybe you need to see her
not as your sister, Row.

"But as a girl. Like you.
Who lost her mother.

"Someone you think you know,
but you don't.

"Someone who isn't going to love you
unconditionally.

"Someone you have to care for.
Feed and water."

"Like friendships," I say.

"Yep. Like friendships."

## Row

I wanted to keep us the same, Ariana and me.
Even after our world had already changed.

But maybe that safety. That lack of evolution.

It kept me from growing. From noticing.
From understanding

that you can't control what you have.

You can only breathe and exist
in the present.

# Ariana

Because part of me knew that to hold this painting.
To hang it against a wall. To create it. To dig down deep,

it meant letting go.

Not only of Mom, but of the part of me
that maybe wanted to remain the girl
who saw her mother die.

I had to let go of being solely defined by that moment.
I had to figure out what happens to the girl
after she leaves the scene.

Because no matter how many miles I traveled,
how many years have passed,
I am still that girl, living in a state of limbo
between the moment my mother lived and my mother died

and as a result, I've become the one hovering
between the moment of life and death.

But this painting, it's my way of saying,
not to the world, but to myself, it's time.

Time to take a deep breath, time to swim
and start to notice what kind of person I am.

Who I can be, not as a girl without a mother,
but as a young woman
who has lived through something
and continues to live through everything.

I unwrap the brown paper from the canvas
and take the painting and center it on the wall.

Then I leave it there hanging
and walk to the other side of the room,
where there are drinks and snacks set out on a table,
and a few of the other students are mingling.

"Hi. I'm Ariana." I outstretch my hand,
and a boy still wearing his beanie and scarf
extends his hand toward me, nodding back at the wall.

"Dope painting."

# Row

We hear an announcement
that the bus is approaching the station.

"What if I can't find her?
What if I do and she doesn't want me?"

Kennedy nods slowly
but doesn't respond.
She takes me in her arms.

An announcement
is telling me to board.

Kennedy squeezes me hard.
"It's gonna be okay,"
she whispers,
and even though so many people
have said this to me
for my entire life,
it feels different coming from Kennedy.

This time it feels true.

# Ariana

I thought that because of the snow, people wouldn't be here.
But they are. The room is alive. Crowded and pulsing.
A middle-aged woman bumps into me. Wine spills on her shawl.
"Sorry," I say to her, and look around for a napkin.

"Don't worry about it," she says. "It was my fault."
She flips the shawl over her shoulder.
The stain lost in the draping.

I watch the parents studying their child's work.
I see siblings growing restless in a room with too many people.
I see Rory and her brother. I see the multicolored-hair girl
in front of her caution tape. I see her wrapping herself
in her caution tape,

and I look toward the door, at the windows outside,
where taxicabs slow and some stop. Where strangers pause
in front of the gallery and consider walking in,

and I see Row, bundled in a thick puffy jacket
and sweatpants, reaching for the door handle,

wanting to be let in.

# Row

I spot her immediately.

Her hair is limp and flat
around the crown,
and dark shadows
hang under her eyes.
But her mouth is stretched
across her face,
and she's laughing.

It's not the image
I anticipated seeing
of my sister.

But I'm not sure
what I was expecting.

She sees me
from across the room
and starts walking toward me.
She's still smiling.

I don't move.

I don't want to ruin
this moment.

I had a lot of time
on the bus down here
to think about what to say.

Her face is neither
happy nor sad
nor perplexed.

It's focused.
Determined.

As she approaches,
my lip starts to quiver.
I bite it hard.
Scrunch my face.
But I can't help it.

There's an arm's length of
distance between us,
but her closeness feels
like she's already touching me.

Then she's there.

"I thought you left me," I cry.
Her arms wrap around me.
Pulling me into her sweater.

Maybe people are staring.
Maybe they've stopped talking.
Maybe they're trying to ignore
the weird girls who are hugging
and crying in the middle of this otherwise
ordinary event.

But I can't tell
what is happening
in the rest of this room,
because Ariana is holding me,
saying, "It's okay."

After a moment, I wriggle
out of her arms, wipe the snot
on the cuff of my sleeve.
Ariana hands me a crumpled napkin.
I blow into it hard.

"Why didn't you tell me
where you went?
I was worried."

Ariana looks at her feet.
Mom used to have the same look
on her face after she missed
yet another one of my games.

The way Mom's face changed
when I asked her
if she could make the next one.

It wasn't a look of guilt or regret.
It was a look of truthfulness.
She wouldn't make it,
because she loved
and was enlivened
by her job.

She wasn't the type of mother
who would schedule around work
or drive her kids to practice.

I know that's why I hold on to her
on the field. Because I want Mom
to be the person who showed up
to my games.

I want to feel her in my heart
each time I strike the ball.

Mom loved us, fiercely,
but she was a person
with hopes and dreams,
fears and flaws,
like her daughters.

I think about
what Kennedy said.

What would I say
to a girl who also
lost her mother?

I wish I had the right words
to say.

People brush past us,
but we can't change
how we feel just because
the room shifts around us.

"I'm scared of losing you.
I'm scared of us changing.
I know that you will someday
leave. I know that we both
will change,
but it's scary."

Ariana doesn't say anything for a moment.
She hesitates to get her words out.

"I'm scared too," she says.
"To let go, to become a person
whose life drifts farther away
from the moment Mom died."

Ariana pauses.
"I'm afraid of being
a bad role model,
a disappointment
to you. I thought
you deserved someone
perfect, but I can't be that."

I snort. "Ariana. I *know*
you're not perfect.
If you were perfect,
you would let me
listen to all of my
soccer podcasts on the way
to school."

Ariana shakes her head.
"Yeah, not gonna happen.
But seriously," she continues,

"I made an eight-year-old cry today.
I said things that hurt him.
It wasn't all that different
from how I might have hurt
you and Dad and Maribel
after learning about the miscarriage.
Or not telling you where I went today."

She pauses. "We have the capacity
to be cruel, if we let the pain consume us.

"But it isn't an excuse. My pain
doesn't give me the right
to inflict pain on someone else.

"I think the truth is,
I wanted to remain the same,
the younger me, frozen in the moment
with too many emotions I didn't know
how to deal with when Mom died,

because I was too scared
to be someone different,
maybe better, maybe changed."

I reach out and hug her.

She smells like
laundry detergent
and pancakes
and sisters.

"We both changed," I say.
"But maybe sometimes
we couldn't see it
in each other,
or in ourselves."

She squeezes me so tight,
and I never want to let her go,
but I know I will have to, someday,

and when it happens
it will be okay.

"Do you want to see my painting?"
Ariana whispers.

I drop my arms and look around the room.
"Yeah. Of course. Why do you think
I'm here?" I smile.

# Ariana

There is a girl around my age standing in front of my painting.
When we get closer, I see a tear running down her cheek.

We stand in front of the painting.
Next to the girl we don't know.

And the more all of us stare at the painting,
the more I feel something.
Eyes stinging. A lump gathering in my throat.
Row wipes at her cheek, and so does the stranger next to us.

Maybe the stranger cries for her mother.
Maybe she cries for her sister.
Maybe she cries for a grandparent or friend.

But it is unmistakable looking at the painting.
When you know grief, you see it too.
In colors. In paintings. In the faces of strangers.

When the stranger senses us standing next to her,
she tries to quickly wipe the tears off her cheek,
but when she looks over at us,
she stops and goes back to looking at the painting
sinking back into her place of feeling
loss and grief and maybe
a sense of understanding.

# Row

There's someone from the gallery,
dressed in all black,
walking around the room,
going up to everyone.

The woman hands me
a sticky-note pad.

"What do you see?"

"Huh?"

She hands me a pen.
"Write it on a sticky note."

She hands one
to the girl standing next to us,
another to Ariana.

I see Mom staring back
at me through
the various shades
of green.

Just like the way
she is on the soccer field.
Except so incredibly different.

Mom is a brushstroke.
Mom is a mix of brown paint.
"She's everywhere," I say quietly.

Ariana's face is surprised.
Like she doesn't realize
that I see her too.

Then she nods at her painting.
"She's here."

I rip off a bright orange
sticky note
and write,
*Mom.*

But the girl next to us,
the stranger,
she scribbles
something too.

She walks up to Ariana's painting
and places her note on the wall,
next to the placard with the title that reads
TURTLE UNDER ICE.

She smooths down the note,
makes sure it sticks,
then moves on
to the next painting.

Ariana and I walk closer
together,

to see what it says,
until we are close enough to read,

*I see hope.*

# Row

There was one winter
it got real cold
in California. So cold
that the ground froze.
The puddles. The ponds.

Bundled in layers of clothes
and thick jackets,
Mom, Ariana, and I
went outside for a walk.

We came across a frozen pond.
Beneath the ice something was trapped.
I pointed to the dark spot in the water.

"A turtle under ice," Mom said.

I crouched down
at the edge of the pond,
the hard ground holding me.
"It lives there?" I asked.

Mom nodded.

"It doesn't hibernate
or bury itself in the mud
or wander south
for the winter?" Ariana asked.

Mom shook her head.
"It stays put in its pond,
breathing underwater."

"Will it die?" I said.

She kissed the top of my head
and squeezed my hand.

"The winter can't stop
a turtle under ice
from swimming,"
she said.

I watched the cross-hatched shell
move so slowly under all that ice.

"No one can stop us
from swimming," I replied.

# Ariana

Maybe not everyone gets my painting.
Maybe they don't see the ice.
Maybe they don't even see the turtle.

I tried to paint it from memory. The refractions of light
under the ice, in colors of green and yellow,
reflections of red.

The large brown lump taking up nearly
the whole canvas. Like you're looking down
on it from above. The way we saw the turtle.

But someone saw something that even I didn't see
in the water, under all that ice.

Maybe hope is like a turtle under ice
breathing through its shell,
through its biochemistry, still alive.

Maybe hope waits for spring to come, for the ice to thaw
for the weight of the pond that encapsulates us
to melt into nothing.

But maybe we are not meant to wait for springtime.
Maybe, instead, we are meant

to break the ice

and be free.

# Acknowledgments

This book was not easy to write, and this one in particular is the result of so much love, support, patience, and understanding of so many people. I am grateful to all my friends and family who stood on the sidelines as cheerleaders through this process, helping this book get here into your hands.

First off, thank you so much to my enormously supportive and patient editor, Jennifer Ung, who read some seriously wild versions of this novel—stuff that will forever be lowered to the bottom of a desk drawer—yet still believing in me and trusting that eventually the heart of the story would come through. The core of the story, the journeys of Ariana and Row, would not have gotten here without your focused attention and dedication.

Secondly, thank you so much to my greatest champion and agent, Brent Taylor. You believe that I can do anything, even when I'm not so sure myself! That support has helped carry me through for this novel. Thank you also to Uwe Stender for helping to bring great things to my work, and everyone at Triada US Literary Agency for the support and enthusiasm.

A very special thank-you to Nova Ren Suma. Thank you for the opportunity to attend Djerassi, and for your guidance, mentorship, and support. For me, Djerassi was truly transformative and will forever shape my future as a writer. The experience allowed me to remember what writing means to me, a love of the craft, process, and the experience of writing. It's something that I must do for myself, whether or not something will ever be published or read by others, and that's okay.

To my fellow writers of Djerassi—Cassie, Heather, Joanna, Kathryn, Mabelle, Naadeyah, Stephanie B., Stephanie F., Sunni, and Tashi—thank you for all the encouragement, feedback, advice, and community you have provided. Also, special shout-out to Tashi for the sticker party, bringing me joy every time I sit down and type on this laptop!

Thank you to Joy McCullough for reading a very early draft of this work and for all the writing and industry advice you've provided. I truly appreciate the time, energy, and support you've offered not just to myself, but to all the writers you mentor and champion. Thank you also to Rachel Lynn Solomon, who encouraged me to pitch the idea of this book to my agent and editor in the first place.

To my critique partners, your advice, writing tips, and craft book recommendations have helped me find a way through some of the tougher parts of this novel. To the Longmont ladies, Susan, Stephanie, Leslie, Eileen, and Penny (reverse couch order this time!).

To the Seattle folks, Ron, Carol, and Corbet. Thank you for the many years of working together and the support throughout.

Finally, to my parents, particularly my mom, who is my best bookseller. My sister. I am so grateful of the life we have as sisters. Being your sister is part of who I am. And to my husband, Steve. I know it was rough at times. Thank you for your patience throughout this whole process.

## About the Author

JULEAH DEL ROSARIO is Chamorro and Filipina and lives in Colorado, where she works as a librarian. She is the author of *500 Words or Less* and *Turtle Under Ice*. Her favorite animal is and always has been a turtle.